SINNER

DI SALLY PARKER

BOOK TEN

M A COMLEY

To my rock, my beautiful mother, who is now watching over me. Dementia sucks. Remembering all the good times we shared together.

You took a huge chunk of my heart with you. Love you and will miss you, until we're reunited once more.

ACKNOWLEDGMENTS

Special thanks as always go to @studioenp for their superb cover design expertise.

My heartfelt thanks go to my wonderful editor Emmy and my proofreaders Joseph and Barbara for spotting all the lingering nits.

Thank you also to my amazing ARC Group who help to keep me sane during this process.

To Mary, gone, but never forgotten. I hope you found the peace you were searching for my dear friend. I miss you each and every day.

ALSO BY M A COMLEY

A Time To Heal (A Sweet Romance)

A Time For Change (A Sweet Romance)

High Spirits

The Temptation series (Romantic Suspense/New Adult Novellas)

Past Temptation

Lost Temptation

Clever Deception (co-written by Linda S Prather)

Tragic Deception (co-written by Linda S Prather)

Sinful Deception (co-written by Linda S Prather)

PROLOGUE

"*G*ather around, men."

The staff congregated in front of Kevin Galen. It was great to see all the familiar faces surrounding him on this job. It had been touch and go there for a while, thanks to the idiotic folks, or how he preferred to call them, 'jobsworths', at the Planning Department, who spent half their day stipulating this, that and the other had to be in place before they could even entertain the commencement of construction on site.

Searching the sea of faces before him, he could tell how relieved the crew were to begin their shift for the day. Kevin outlined what he expected from them, nothing different to the countless jobs they'd embarked upon before, when they'd worked together.

"There it is in a neat nutshell. Let's get cracking. I'll be around for the rest of the day should anyone need me. Good luck. Let's get the machines running at full pelt, at least try our best to get the project back on some form of bloody workable schedule."

The men smiled, nodded, and some of the younger ones

1

even high-fived each other before they left the area. The welcome sound of heavy machinery filling the air was music to Kevin's ears after months of daily negotiations with the planners. They'd forced him to perform several circus acts to get this particular show on the road.

The row of cottages was in dire need of demolition now, after a gas explosion had torn through them around six months before. Kevin had earmarked the site as a potential area to erect a block of flats. Some members of the planning council had agreed it was the way to go to in order to ease the lack of housing in the community, while there were various objectors, determined to keep things as they were in that particular part of the countryside. While he sympathised with the objectors on a personal front, as a builder and businessman, he was also fully aware of the need for regeneration with the view to adding more bodies per square metre to a project, to fulfil the need to get people on benefits out of local hotels et cetera.

He entered the Portakabin and settled down behind his desk, as usual, a pile of paperwork awaiting him. Everything was going to plan until the noise of the site died down around lunchtime. Kevin thought this was strange; most of the men tended to bring lunch with them and insisted on eating it on the go, eager to keep to their tight schedule. He sat there for an extra few minutes and dealt with another email, distracted by the silence to the extent that he could no longer stand it.

Opening the door, the sun's rays hitting him full force, he strained to see across the site and shielded his eyes from the glare. Over to the edge of the plot was a group of men, all pointing and staring at something in front of them. Kevin tore down the steps and blazed a trail through the heavy plant equipment to see for himself what the dickens was going on.

"Everything all right here, men?"

"Umm... I was just about to come and fetch you, Kev, to see what you made of this," Harry, his foreman, stated.

While he'd been in his office the cottages had been knocked down and the rubble cleared away. Puzzled, Kevin's gaze shifted from Harry's hefty frame to the ground that had been turned over by the huge digger. Unsure what he was looking at, he took several steps closer to the hole. There was no mistaking it, not now. The sandwich he'd been nibbling on in the office was threatening to re-emerge. He stared at Harry and whispered, "What the fuck do we do?"

"We need to call the police, let them deal with it. However, this is the bad part: I know from past experience, the frigging site will be shut down."

Kevin ran a hand through his short dark hair. "Fuck, that's all we need." He leaned in and lowered his voice. "I suppose ignoring it is out of the question?"

Harry raised an eyebrow. "I know you're under pressure to get this site cleared, boss, but yes, that would be out of the question. They're human bones."

Kevin kicked out at several of the stones close to his feet, spun away from the skeleton that he knew would blight his life for weeks, if not months to come, and let out a thunderous yell of frustration.

The crew all stared at him, most of them wearing sympathetic expressions, but there was the odd frown of disbelief thrown into the mix, as well.

"Okay, gents, we need to down tools for the day until someone official gets here." He stomped back to the cabin, the men's groans of irritation following him. Inside, he took a few moments to get his own frustration under control before he eventually walked over to the desk to place the call.

"Yes, police, please. I've found the remains of a dead body." He closed his eyes and shook his head over and over as the operator bombarded him with questions he simply couldn't answer. "Look, all I know is that we started digging on site this morning, and a few hours into the excavation process, my men have unearthed what appears to be human remains, hence the reason why I'm making this call. Do with it what you will, I can't say anything else about the situation."

"Okay, sir. I'm merely following procedure."

"And now you're expecting me to apologise to you? It ain't going to happen, lady. Do what you have to do and let us get back to work ASAP."

"For your information, the site will be closed down immediately."

"For how long?"

"That will depend on the authorities concerned, sir. Leave it with me, I'll arrange for an officer to attend right away."

"Gee, thanks. How to ruin my day in one bloody sentence. How long are they likely to be?"

"They should be with you soon, depending on who's available."

Kevin ended the call and threw the phone back on the desk. He moved over to the window and glanced out at the men milling around, close to the corpse. "This just about sums up my year, finding this bloody thing on top of getting a divorce and losing access to my kids." He raised his gaze skywards. "What else do you intend throwing at me?"

CHAPTER 1

*S*ally beamed, seeing Jack Blackman, her former partner, poking his head around the door to her office. "Hello, you. What brings you here today? Never mind that, how are you? Come in, sit down."

"I don't want to disturb you. I know how damn busy you can be day in and day out, and no, I don't miss all the tension and drama that goes on around here."

She gestured for him to sit opposite her, and he smiled.

"It's great seeing you and the others. I've missed not being around, well, kind of. Some things I'll never miss, like making you a cup of coffee when you've got a cob on."

"Bollocks, that never happened. It must be your imagination playing tricks on you. Genuinely, it's great to see you up and about again. How are the physio sessions going?"

"Don't ask. Sometimes I swear I know what a victim goes through who has been trussed up and tortured for days on end before we've come along and set them free."

Sally laughed. "I doubt if that's true. How's the family coping with having you around full-time?"

"You mean, hanging around their necks like a tightened noose?"

She grinned. "Yeah, that as well."

"I'm driving them potty. Donna has told me to get a hobby, take up golf or something inane like that, and quickly. Long gone is all the sympathy they showered me with when I first had my accident."

"Poor you. They love you really. Seriously, what do you intend to do now you're a man of leisure on a healthy police pension?"

"Healthy? If that's what you think during a cost-of-living crisis that is getting harder and harder each day to overcome. Oops... sorry, I swore to Donna I would never get on my soapbox about that subject again."

"Yes, I'm with Donna on that one. No point dwelling on it, Jack. It's up to the powers that be to sort it out. We need to be thankful we're in the middle of summer now and not having to find extra money to cover all the heating bills."

"Yeah, that's what Donna keeps telling me. She's busy squirreling money away to cover the bills in the winter, not something I would ever think about doing. Well, we've never had to sink to that level in the past."

"That's why women are invaluable around the home, we manage all the bills without you men having to deal with such mundane tasks. We're great organisers, most of the time, figuring out what's on the menu daily, sorting out the washing and ironing and every other major thing that helps to keep the household ticking over nicely."

He cocked an eyebrow and asked, "Tell me, when was the last time you had to do any of that shit?"

Sally frowned, scratched her head and twisted her mouth from side to side. "Umm... admittedly, not that often now that I'm married to Simon. He tends to keep the house running like a well-oiled machine, but I have my moments, been known to pull my weight around the house now and again."

He lifted his eyebrow once more, coughed and said, "Bullshit!"

Sally screwed up a used brown envelope lying to the side of her and threw it at him. "You, cheeky sod. Why don't you go on a course to learn something useful?" She clicked her thumb and forefinger together. "I know, enrol in a cookery course at the college."

"Never, not in a bloody million years. I have a reputation to consider with my mates."

"Jesus, I've heard it all now. Donna told me at the hospital, you've never once made her a meal, not even beans on toast."

"That's right, and I'm proud of it. It's not the man's place to spend hours in the kitchen, picking up crippling burns, risking the hairs on his arms, while cooking for his family."

"Christ, you really do live in the Dark Ages, don't you? I'll get Simon to give you some lessons, if you like. He adores cooking, sees it as a pleasure, not a sodding chore."

"He's different. He had to fend for himself for years until you two started dating."

"Is that the only reason you married Donna? Because she could find her way around the kitchen without resorting to using a compass?"

He smiled smugly and winked. "Yep. Next question?"

Sally spread her hands over the desk. "As you can see, I have a shitload of work to keep me occupied, so, as much as I would love to spend the next few hours pointing out where you've gone wrong in your marriage, it's not going to happen."

He wiped his brow. "Thank fuck for that." He winced as he rose from his seat.

"Are you all right? Should you be out and about so soon?"

"I needed to collect my stuff before the end of the week.

Anyway, I wanted to invite you and the rest of the team to the pub this evening, for my leaving do."

"For the obligatory orange juice in your case," she teased.

"Yep, I'm totally off the drink, haven't touched a drop since the accident. Not worth the bloody risk, take my word for it."

"Don't, I still feel guilty you didn't join me and Lorne that night at the pub."

He wagged a finger. "No regrets. I don't have any, so why should you? It was an accident, it could have happened anytime. Well, are you coming or what?"

"Of course I will. We'll be sure to give you a good send-off Jack, we're all going to miss your mardiness around here."

"Bloody charming, that is. I'll see you over the road at six then, or thereabouts. Will it be all right if I bring Donna along? She's keen to meet everyone properly and to show her appreciation to you all for the kindness you've shown me over the last few months."

"Goes without saying."

There was a knock on the door, and it eased open. Lorne poked her head into the room. "Sorry for interrupting you, we've had a call about a skeleton being discovered at a building site."

Sally rolled her eyes. "Sounds ominous."

"Well, ladies, that's my call to leave. I'll see you both over the road later, if you can make it."

"We'll do our absolute best, Jack. It's been great to see you again, glad your recovery is going well. Don't be a stranger, will you? I'm always on the end of the phone if you ever need a chat," Sally replied. She left her seat and gave her former partner a hug.

She was surprised at the strength of Jack's embrace in return which almost left her breathless.

"Thanks, Sally, for everything. You've been the greatest boss and friend over the years."

She placed a hand on his forehead. "Are you sure you're feeling okay?"

All three of them laughed, and Sally's eyes filled up with unexpected tears.

"Now look what you've gone and done."

He bent and kissed her on the cheek. "You're one in a million, Sally Parker-Bracknall."

Her cheeks heated up. "Get out of here. I can't cope with you heaping all these compliments on me, it's unprecedented." She shoved him gently towards the door and watched him take his first tentative steps back out into the incident room to collect the box filled with his belongings. "Jordan, do me a favour and carry that box out to Jack's car, will you?"

Jack turned and said, "I can do it, I'm not an inval... id. Or maybe I am. All right, just this once, if it's okay with you, Jordan?"

"It's fine, boss... er, Jack. It'll be my pleasure."

Lorne nudged Sally. "You'll see him again. Don't show him how upset you are."

"Yeah, I know. Anyway, we can't hang around here. Where's the site?"

"Out at Watton."

"We'd better get over there. You can fill me in with the details on the way. I'll just grab my jacket, not that I'll probably need it."

"You won't, it's a blistering hot day out there, not that we've seen much of it today. You're going to be grateful if a breeze gets up."

They followed Jordan and Jack out to the car.

Jordan placed the box in the boot of Jack's vehicle and shook his hand. "See you later, mate. I'll buy you your first pint of orange juice." He chuckled and made his way back into the station.

Sally and Lorne both hugged Jack, then Sally held the driver's door open for him and watched him gingerly lower himself into the car.

"I'm sure it'll get easier the more physio sessions you attend. Make sure you take everything on offer, Jack. I know how damn stubborn you can be at times."

"Me?" he asked, his hand flattened over his chest. "I think you must be mistaken."

Sally shook her head and bent to give him another kiss. "You've got this, big man. Don't be a stranger, you've been like a brother to me over the years."

It was Jack's turn to tear up. "That's what I'm going to miss the most, being with you every day. All right, most days you were like a thorn in my side, but there was the odd occasion when you made me smile with one of your dreadful jokes, now and again."

"Gee, thanks, I'll take that as a compliment. We'll see you later. Love to Donna and the girls. Will they be joining us this evening?"

"I doubt it. You know what bloody teenagers are like when it comes to hanging out with their folks."

"Glad I was never like that. I loved going on adventures with my parents, still do."

He nodded and started the engine. Sally closed the door and waved at him as he reversed out of the space.

Lorne tugged on her arm. "Back to work, boss."

"I don't mind admitting that a piece of my heart has gone with him, Lorne."

"I'd be shocked if it hadn't. Hey, at least your partner, or should I say ex-partner, is still around."

Sally grimaced. "Sorry, I'm being totally selfish. I never thought about what you must be going through right now."

"Don't worry about me. I know Pete died years ago, but I still find myself having conversations with him. How daft is that?"

"You're bound to. Come on, let's shake a leg."

AFTER DRIVING IN RELATIVE SILENCE, each of them feeling in a reflective mood during the journey, Lorne pointed out the site as they approached. There had been a few new estates erected in the area over the past ten or twenty years.

"Ah, I see. It's this one here, not the main one at the top, which I thought it was going to be," Lorne said. "I remember reading about this place a few months ago. I think there were four cottages and they were earmarked to be demolished due to a gas explosion which took place in one of the middle cottages."

"Oh heck. That scenario is a nightmare in itself. Let's hope we're able to track down the previous owners without much hassle."

"You read my mind."

"Let's see what we've got first and then assess where we go from there. Looks like Pauline and her team have already made a start."

Sally pointed out the slim-built pathologist speaking with a bunch of techs in white paper suits, her blonde spiky hair standing to attention and perfectly still in spite of the slight breeze that was circulating the open area.

Sally locked the car, and she and Lorne walked over to catch the end of what Pauline was telling her team.

"We go over everything. Take as many samples as we can. Don't be put off by the workmen, they're bound to be pissed off with our presence. Now, off you go."

The techs departed, and Pauline retrieved her bag from the back of the van.

"Hi, Paul. How's it going?" Sally announced their arrival.

"Christ, where did you pop up from? You scared the crap out of me."

Sally sniggered. "Didn't you see us lingering at the back of the pack?"

"You seriously think I'd be asking if I did? Be still my racing heart."

"You can be such a drama queen." Sally bit down on her tongue after realising she didn't really know Pauline well enough to be calling her names, even in jest.

"Yeah, well, as it happens, my ma used to say the same, God rest her soul," Pauline replied, her gaze drifting to the ground between them.

Suffering from a huge bout of guilt, Sally said, "I'm sorry, I didn't know your mother was dead."

"She died when I was a kid. I was brought up by my father and his second wife, my evil stepmother. She used to beat me with a metal pole and lock me in the cupboard under the stairs, only let me out when my father's car pulled into the drive. I had a terrible, abusive childhood that I wouldn't wish on my worst enemy."

Sally rubbed Pauline's arm in sympathy and swallowed down the lump that had appeared in her throat. "How awful. I didn't mean to bring back any bad memories for you, Paul."

Pauline shrugged and smiled. "You haven't, I'm winding you up. Both my parents are alive and kicking, more's the pity in my father's case. He's a selfish, attention-seeking toerag, but my mother worships the ground he walks on, so my opinion of the tosser doesn't really matter, does it?"

Unsure how to react to the pathologist's latest revelation, Sally chewed on her lip and cast a glance in Lorne's direction for help.

Sadly, none was forthcoming, and the three of them all stared at each other until Pauline broke into a fit of giggles.

"I'm kidding. God, ladies, you truly have a lot to learn about me, don't you?"

"I think we've got the gist of what a wind-up merchant you can be. Glad you feel comfortable enough with us now to consider taking the piss, especially when our professionalism is most needed at a crime scene."

Pauline's eyes narrowed, and she wagged a finger, inches from Sally's face. "Ah, you're presuming it's a crime scene."

"Oops! When a body turns up buried, unless it's situated in a graveyard, I would have thought the most obvious assumption would be that person died from foul play. I'll await your expert opinion before I go down that route instead, shall I?"

"You'd be wise to, yes. Anyway, my team and I have lots to embark upon before we can even entertain removing the remains from the site, therefore, I believe you can do us both an enormous favour by having a word with the person running this project. I'm getting the impression he's far from happy with the discovery. You might also warn him about the likely outcome of him causing any unnecessary grief for me and my crew in your absence."

"If that's what you want. And if he asks how long you're likely to be here? What shall I tell him?"

"That it will take as long as it needs to, end of. You might also like to remind him that patience is a virtue," Pauline added doggedly.

"Shit!" Sally glanced over at a couple of men standing on the top of the Portakabin steps. One man in particular had her in his sights, she could tell. She turned her back on him in case he could lip-read what she was about to say next. "How to ruin someone's week during a conversation. I just know this isn't going to go down well."

"Hey, there's no point working yourself up into a state, Sally," Lorne whispered.

Sally faced her. "Isn't there? Look at us, three women, all perceived to be doing a man's role in this world. You know how welcome that type of news goes down with some men."

Lorne's head jutted forward. She rubbed the back of it after it cracked. "Sod it! Seriously? Surely those days are long behind us now, aren't they?"

Pauline heaved out a sigh. "I fear Sally could be spot on with her assumption. That's the impression I got after spending two minutes in the man's presence when I arrived and made him aware what the procedures were in a case like this."

"Great, you've already told him what's what and he's still intent on giving us the evil eye—no, don't look. He's glaring over here. I'm surprised we're still standing, the number of daggers being fired in our direction right now."

"Don't, really. Now I'm tempted to have a sneaky peek," Lorne said on the back of a nervous giggle.

"I'm sorry to dump this on your doorstep, ladies, but if you don't mind, I need to get on. I can't stand my team hanging around, doing fuck all, when there's a corpse or remains to be dealt with. We're awaiting the arrival of a forensic archaeologist as well, just to make you aware."

"Makes sense to request their attendance. We'll catch up with you soon. Should we wear a suit when we eventually join you? Is it worth it?"

Pauline stared at her and cocked an eyebrow. "I'll pretend you didn't say that. Always, at any scene of mine, where your assistance is required. Are we clear on that, Inspector?"

"We are. I'll consider myself suitably reprimanded. We'll catch up with you soon."

"Good luck in your task. I fear yours is going to be a far tougher one than ours, and yes, that was a joke."

"Forgive me if I refrain from laughing."

"You're forgiven. I must get on, as should you." With that,

Pauline marched towards the rest of her team who were busy sorting out their equipment, her oversized suit rustling with every step.

"She's certainly coming out of her shell around us," Lorne noted.

"Yeah, I'm noncommittal about whether that's a good or bad thing. I'll tell you later what the outcome is. Let's get this over and done with." Sally started the walk towards the Portakabin and noticed one of the men speak to the other, hiding his mouth behind his hand. "This looks ominous. Back me up if you sense me struggling to get my point across. You know what I went through with Darryl all those years."

"Shit, I'd forgotten all about that. I've got your back, don't worry, Sal. Think positive and stay strong, shoulders back at all times."

Sally smiled. "Thanks, partner. That was my intention, it's whether I can maintain it that's worrying me."

"You're stronger than you think. You've overcome so much in your life this far, dealing with this cretin, if he gives you any trouble, should be a doddle."

"Thanks. We'll see about that. Here goes." Sally consciously set a smile in place to disguise how churned up her insides were, but not only that, going by past experience, she knew how disarming a smile could be in the face of adversity. "Hi, I take it one of you two gents is the person in charge around here. I'm Detective Inspector Sally Parker, and this is my partner, Detective Sergeant Lorne Warner."

"Yes, this is my site. I'm Kevin Galen. First off, you can tell me just how long construction is going to be held up with this shit."

Sally raised an eyebrow. The man's tone got her back up, and she inhaled a sneaky breath to calm herself. "This shit… could be a murder scene. Of course, we're not likely to know that until the pathologist and her team have carried out a thorough examination of the area. Unfortunately, that could take days, weeks, or in some cases, even months."

Galen's eyes blazed, and he craned his neck forward at the same time he ran a hand through his thick, mid-brown hair. "What the fuck! This site has been doomed since the day I put my money on the table. Jesus, months, you say? That's unthinkable. It means I can wave goodbye to any kind of profit I was expecting. Shit! Why me? Why now?"

"Would you rather discuss this privately, Mr Galen? Inside, perhaps?"

He patted the other man on his back and sent him on his way then crashed through the doorway to the cabin. The door swung back and forth on its hinges a few times before Sally stopped it and entered with Lorne bringing up the rear. They found Galen leaning back in his chair, his hands on top of his head, behind a cluttered desk.

"I can only apologise, Mr Galen, and ask you to put yourself in the deceased's family's shoes. If that was a member of your family out there, you'd expect the appropriate authorities to deal with the investigation correctly, wouldn't you?"

"I know you're right. However, I've got a damn business to run, with a tight schedule that has been severely impacted by the negligence of the local planning office. I was hoping the rest of the build would be plain sailing. Dumb, I know. Within a few hours of starting the excavations, this frigging nightmare turns up and puts a massive spanner in the works. My mind is all over the shop right now. My prime concern is where I'm going to come up with the funds to deal with this blasted delay. The men will have to be paid, whether they're on site or not, if I intend keeping this project viable. If they leave and start working somewhere else, there's no telling who I'll be able to call upon to complete the build. These are tough times we're living in regarding the building trade,

Inspector. So forgive me if I'm a tad pissed off about finding a skeleton slap bang in the middle of my million-pound-plus development."

Sally smiled tautly. "Wow, that much, eh? What are you building here?"

"A block of fifty-six flats."

"And how long is that likely to take to complete?" Sally asked.

Galen sat upright and glared at her. "You tell me, now we've come a cropper."

"Ordinarily, what type of timescale would we be looking at?"

"A year tops. Although that's a guesstimate. We usually factor in the odd slip-up here and there, but nothing of this magnitude. Now you're telling me your guys might well be around for a few months yet, putting the kibosh on any schedule I might be working to. Not what I needed to hear at this stage in my life, I can tell you."

Sally frowned and inclined her head. "Care to enlighten us as to what you mean by that?"

"Let's just say I was hoping this place, and the fortune it's likely to generate at the end, would make up for what I've lost this year so far."

"I'm not with you," Sally replied.

"My marriage, my kids, I've lost the lot. I left the family home, and this job was supposed to be the clean break I needed to start rebuilding my life. A cat in hell's chance of that happening now, thanks to this debacle."

"Ah, I see, that explains why you're so irate."

"Irate? Yes, I'm irate, too bloody right I am. I'm absolutely livid. Mortified that the site has come to an abrupt halt through no fault of my own. And here you are, telling me that we could be out of action for bloody months. I'm trying hard to deal with that prospect and failing miserably. Sorry if you're taking the brunt of my frustration, it is what it is. I've been on a downer all year, and this just happens to be the cherry on top of the sodding cake in my opinion."

Sally pulled up a chair from the side of the room and positioned it in front of his desk. Lorne did the same, although she had to clear her seat of rolled-up plans first.

"Just bung them on the floor, they're pretty much worthless now anyway," Galen told Lorne.

"Aren't you insured?" Sally asked.

Galen puffed out his cheeks and picked up a pen which he twisted through his slender fingers that Sally guessed hadn't seen any form of manual work for years, if ever. "I couldn't afford it, premiums have skyrocketed lately on sites like this, just like everything else in this country. Damn Brexit, sodding government... nope, I'm not going there. All politicians are a waste of space in my opinion, always have been. Honest folk are out there, busting a gut, trying hard to make a living, and all the time these effing politicians are taking backhanders and breaking the law left, right and centre. Not a day goes by without one of them being in the headlines for something or other. Why don't they put their heads down and get on with the job they're being paid to do? There's a novelty, right? And don't get me started on the PM and his billionaire wife. Then there's all this trouble with the police these days, look at the shambles the Met is in. Christ Almighty, what the frigging hell is this country coming to with all this crap to deal with? Let alone the cost of the state funerals and the king's coronation, I dread to think how much that lot set back the taxpayers. It's never-ending, and then you've got the likes of me, doing all he can to make ends meet, and I get lumbered with this farcical situation. Holy crap! You couldn't make this sort of shit up, could you?"

Sally sat back and let the man chunter on, secretly agreeing with most of the points he had raised, although she would never admit as much. "Anyway, getting back to the hand we've been dealt today. We're going to need more information about the site."

"Such as?"

"Who you bought it from? Am I right in thinking there was a row of cottages here before the demolition began?"

"Yes, that's right, four cottages."

"And you bought the site as a job lot, or did you have to purchase each of the homes individually?"

"Individually. Thankfully, all the owners agreed to sell. The homes were in an appalling state; the insurance would have paid out, if the owners were insured, that is. Daft not to be, especially if you live in a semi or terrace. A gas explosion happened at number four. That cottage was virtually destroyed, not possible to salvage any of it, so it made sense to condemn the rest of the cottages and start over."

"Except your intention is to build a block of flats. Did you have to jump through a lot of hoops with the Planning Department to obtain the necessary approval?"

"And some. It's been a nightmare project from the outset. I didn't have much to do with the sale of the properties. I viewed them with Taylors Estate Agents and then left the rest of it up to my solicitor to sort out."

Lorne withdrew her notebook and jotted down the relevant information.

"And your solicitor is?" Sally asked. She was far more relaxed now than when the interview had commenced.

"Franks and Partridge. I've got a card here somewhere." He opened the top drawer in his desk, flung a few items around and removed a card which he slid towards Lorne.

Lorne noted down the number and smiled. "Thanks, that's really helpful."

She returned the card, and Galen popped it back in the drawer.

"I really don't know the ins and outs about who owned the properties, it's not something that really interested me. All I set out to do was get my hands on the site."

"It's okay, I'm sure your solicitor will be able to fill in the blanks for us," Sally said. "Have you seen anyone nosing around the site who had no right to be here? Anyone taking a special interest perhaps?"

He contemplated the question for a few seconds and then shook his head. "I don't think so. We've been around for the last week or so, getting the site ready, you know, putting up the fencing, making sure everything is legally secure, as is our responsibility these days. To be honest, I've been focused on that side of things more than what the neighbours or passers-by have been up to."

Sally strained her neck and peered out of the window at the row of cottages across the street and made a mental note to check them out once they were finished with Galen.

"I know the pathologist and her guys haven't had a chance to really do an in-depth examination of the remains, but did she give you any indication how long it had been down there?" He shuddered after asking his question.

"In my experience, it's far too early to even give a rough guesstimate of the timescale. Is there anything else you can tell us about the site that you think might be useful to the investigation? Any idea where the remains were found, under which property?"

His shoulders rose and fell. "I haven't got the foggiest, I was too shocked to notice. I've been that focused on getting this site up and running, all that has come back and bit me hard in the arse today. All I can tell you is that there were four cottages, numbered alternately, going back and forth across the road. The cottages on the demolished side were two, four, six and eight, not sure if that helps or not?"

"Thanks, it's a start. All I can do is apologise for the

inconvenience. These things are sent to try us at the best of times."

"After the divorce went through, I sensed my luck was about to change. That is why this project means so much to me. If you can give me a hand, Inspector, to get the construction back on track ASAP, I'll be forever in your debt."

"Again, I apologise. Unfortunately, that decision is out of my hands. I will do my best but I wouldn't hold out much hope of them getting the job done within the next week or so."

"Great. I was half expecting you to say that, although it still sucks."

"You say the area has been secured; who has access to the keys?"

"Me and my foreman. Saying that, I've only just handed him a bunch this morning. Why?"

"Have you left the keys unattended at all?"

He dug his hand in his pocket and withdrew a bunch. "Nope, they're with me day and night. What are you getting at?"

"I wondered what the likelihood would be of anyone gaining access to the area, that's all."

"What? To dump the body?" He shook his head. "That doesn't make sense, the body was buried four to five feet under concrete, or had you forgotten that fact?"

Sally nodded. "Just trying to think outside the box. Okay, if there's nothing else, we'd better get on with the investigation."

"Yes, I think that would be for the best. Here's my card. Can you ring me straight away when you're given the all-clear to open up the site again? Seriously, time is money, and every minute of every day matters."

"You have my word. Thanks for speaking with us. Again, apologies for the disruption."

"I suppose it is what it is at the end of the day. I don't blame you per se, I'm angry with the universe for testing my resilience yet again. It just seems it's been one thing after another this year, and I'm sick to death of dealing with the devastating consequences."

"I'm sure. Take care. Hopefully I'll be in touch soon."

Sally and Lorne both rose from their seats and walked towards the door while Galen remained at his desk, his gaze drifting out of the window, staring at the sky.

"See, that went far better than you were anticipating, didn't it?" Lorne said the second they left the cabin.

"Yeah, I suppose it just goes to show the confidence I had with Jack standing alongside me."

"As opposed to a feeble female like me, you mean?"

"Ouch! I didn't mean it to come across like that, or are you guilty of twisting my bloody words again?"

"Whatever. I think I know what you're getting at. Going forward, there are bound to be times when, as two female officers, we feel threatened. The key is not to let the buggers see or sense our apprehension."

"Is that how you managed it after Pete died, you know, taking on Katy as your partner?"

"Honestly, it never even crossed my mind. I've never felt any insecurity in my role, having a female partner alongside me."

"Whoa, okay, that told me. In other words, I need to give myself the proverbial kick up the jacksy and get on with it, right?"

Lorne grinned. "You said it, not me."

"Let's get suited up and go see the gruesome discovery for ourselves."

Lorne groaned. "If we must. There's always a major downside to investigating a cold case, and nine times out of ten it usually comes down to staring at a skeleton."

Sally tilted her head. "Don't tell me you're squeamish?"

"All right, I won't, except I am, especially when confronted with a bag of bones. I remember one day in biology at school, Wayne Raddon chasing me around the science lab with the skeleton that used to reside in the corner. I don't mind telling you I've had a phobia about them ever since."

"Crap, hardly ideal in our line of business."

"Yeah, but to be fair, most victims I had to deal with in the Met had their skin still attached. Okay, they might have had the odd limb missing here and there."

"Which you didn't mind?"

"Nope. Call me weird, if you like."

"Nah, we all have things that set off our gag reaction now and again."

Sally removed two suits from the boot of the car and handed one to Lorne.

Slipping hers on, Lorne asked, "What's yours?"

Sally racked her brains and jumped up and down on the spot to ensure her suit was snug in all the right places. "I'm sure there must be something but I can't for the life of me think of anything right now. You probably trump me on the gruesome crimes. I bet you seen it all, living in London. In our neck of the woods, the crimes tend to be more subdued, shall we say?"

"I call dealing with a bag of stripped bones just about as gruesome as it gets."

"You're not going to pull a Jack on me and vomit everywhere, are you?"

"I can't make promises I might break once confronted with the skeleton." Lorne zipped up her suit, and her cheeks coloured up.

"We could be looking at an interesting few minutes or hours ahead of us."

"Oh God, I hope it's the former and not the latter... just saying."

Sally chuckled and led the way across the road to where Pauline and her team were completing their set-up procedures.

"Any luck?" Pauline asked. She nodded towards the Portakabin off to their right.

"Not really. We've got the name of the estate agent and the solicitor to chase up, but that's about it."

"Joy of joys. I wouldn't want to be in your shoes."

"How's it going here, or is that too much to ask at this stage?"

"You guessed right. Hey, your partner is looking a bit peaky there," Pauline stated, her eyes narrowed in Lorne's direction.

"She doesn't do skeletons."

"What?" Pauline screeched. "A hardened former Met officer on the brink of puking... over a *skeleton?*"

Lorne stared at her. "There's no need to rub it in. I'm just warning you that I might need to run if it gets too bad."

"Maybe you should consider a different career if that's how you react to seeing a dead body," Pauline muttered.

Sally stifled a giggle as Lorne mimicked the newbie pathologist behind her back. "If we can get back to business, ladies? Are there any obvious injuries yet?"

"Having only had the chance to examine the remains briefly, nothing noticeable so far. We're almost set up. You're going to need to be patient with us on this one."

Sally shuffled forward a few paces and stared at the skeleton. "Can you tell if we're dealing with a male or female yet?"

"What part of 'you're going to need to be patient' didn't you understand?" Pauline responded abruptly.

"Sorry, shame on me. I'm eager to get to the bottom of the case, it's a major failing of mine." She grinned and took a step back to allow the photographer to fire off some shots.

Lorne clutched Sally's arm. "I'm sorry, I'm going to have to…" She took off towards the car and made it to the edge of the cordon before she threw up.

"You need to have a word with her," Pauline insisted.

"I don't, it's fine. Some people have weaker stomachs than others. She'll be okay. Just ignore her."

"That's hard to do if she's vomiting all over a possible crime scene."

Sally rolled her eyes up to the fluffy clouds that had gathered, which gave them some reprieve from the intense heat. "And I can do without the extra hassle this situation is causing."

"Pardon me for speaking my mind. I'll get back to work then, shall I?"

Sally turned her back on the pathologist and saw Lorne heading her way. "Are you okay now or still a bit queasy?"

"I think I'll be fine, if I don't look at it again."

"You can turn your back on it, I'd still value your input."

Sally thought she heard Pauline tut but chose to ignore it. She and Lorne remained quiet for the next ten minutes or so, allowing Pauline breathing space to make her preliminary assessment.

It wasn't until Pauline stood and shook out her legs that Sally asked her first question, "What are your initial thoughts?"

"In all honesty, it's hard to tell in situ if the victim is male or female. Now, if you were to really push me for an answer, I would say… it's a male."

"Okay, that's a start, but is it enough for us to go on? When will you have a definitive answer for us?"

"By the end of the day would be my rough estimate. As for COD, that's impossible to say at this time. Having briefly inspected the remains, there's a fracture to the skull, but who's to say when that happened? It could have been when the body was buried in the concrete or possibly during the excavation. I'm inclined to believe it's the former."

"No other injuries that you can tell?"

"You're pushing me unnecessarily, Inspector. These things take time to assess. Why don't you let us proceed with our job? I'm sure we'll get on a lot quicker without your involvement at this point in the proceedings."

"In other words, you want us to bugger off and leave you to it?"

Pauline grinned. "I'll be in touch with my report as and when."

"Okay, we'll get to it and do the necessary digging…"

Pauline lifted her hand. "You don't have to fill me in, you have your job and we have ours, let's not blur the line." She then turned her attention to her team once more and gave each member a specific task to carry out.

Sally backed away, feeling like she had been dismissed. Lorne joined her.

"She's right," Sally said, "we should crack on with our side of the investigation."

"I agree. Where do you want to start? With the solicitor or the estate agent?"

Sally's gaze drifted across the road to the row of cottages opposite. "Neither. I think we should knock on a few doors around here first. I've already spotted some curtain twitching going on. Odds are that someone will know something of use to get us underway. Let's get out of these suits. Another waste of money, considering how long we've been in them."

They began the walk back to the car.

"It's a necessity," Lorne said, "although I have to agree with you querying having to put one on in the first place, given that we're on a building site and the person has obviously been dead for years, so any evidence available will be questionable."

"That was my thought process but them's the breaks. You must be relieved not to be hanging around here for too long."

"Yep, you took the words out of my mouth. How do you want to play this? Split up or stick together?"

Slipping out of her suit at the cordon and popping it in the awaiting black sack, Sally replied, "I think we'll cover more ground quicker if we split up."

Lorne placed her suit in the sack and nodded. "Absolutely."

"Go along the lines that we don't know what gender the victim is and see where that leads you. It appears to be a quiet neighbourhood, so there's every chance someone will be able to give us an insight into who lived there and when."

"It's a shame we haven't got a rough estimate as to how long the victim has been buried."

"It's the hand we've been dealt, it's up to us to carry out the necessary digging to see what treasures we can find."

"It's got to be better than uncovering that particular treasure." Lorne jerked a thumb over her shoulder.

They both chuckled. There were six cottages in total, and once they reached them, Lorne started at one end and Sally walked the length of the row and began at the other. Sally knocked on the first door and stood there for a while, but the door remained unanswered. She hadn't noticed anyone in the cottage earlier, unlike next door. Her gaze drifted to the neighbouring cottage and spotted the slight movement in the curtain, more than if the fabric had been shifted by the breeze on this side of the road.

Sally left the tiny front garden of the first cottage and made her way up the two steps to the front door of the neighbour's. She rang the bell and, not long after, a wizened old lady with short grey hair answered the door.

Sally showed her ID. "Hello there, sorry to disturb you. I'm DI Sally Parker of the Norfolk Constabulary. Would it be possible to have a quick word with you?"

"About what's going on over the road?"

"That's right. Can I come in?"

"Why can't you do it here? I don't like strangers coming into my house uninvited. Just because I'm retired, I stick to doing my chores on certain days. That means I'm supposed to do the hoovering tomorrow."

Sally smiled, her aim to overcome the woman's snarky tone. "I won't judge, I promise."

"Your lot always judge, so don't give me that crap."

Sally removed her notebook from her pocket and flipped it open at a new page. "First of all, may I ask your name?"

"Moira Lamont."

"And how long have you lived here?"

"All my married life, so that would be coming up to nearly fifty years. There's only me left now, my husband died three years ago of a heart attack. It was expected, so don't bother showing me any sympathy. The old bugger never sat still, lived on his nerves, that one. Spent most of his days in the 'man shed' he built at the bottom of the garden. It suited me. Funny, though, I never thought I'd miss him but on the odd occasion I do."

"You're bound to after spending so many years together. I'm sorry for your loss. Do you have any children?"

"No. I never wanted them, I've never had a maternal bone in my body."

"I'm the same."

A smile appeared on the old woman's face. "It's not all it is cracked up to be, you know, being a mother. I went through hell when I was first married. Everyone around me kept

28

asking why I hadn't fallen pregnant. I was made to feel like an outcast when I told them I had no intention of having any children. Stan, my hubby, he never wanted them either. I've always been one for animals, though. I've got a cat, she's old now, but she's the purrfect companion for me."

Sally laughed. "I see what you did there. I agree, I have a nutty-as-a-fruitcake golden Labrador called Dex. He's my world."

Mrs Lamont wagged her finger. "I'm sorry, I don't agree with people owning dogs if they're out at work all day."

"In my defence, I've never left him alone. My parents used to look after him during the day, and now my husband works from home, kind of, they're together all the time."

"Ah, then you must forgive me for speaking out of turn, I'm sorry."

"Don't be, it's fine. I happen to agree with you on that score, too. Must be hard for dogs in particular being left all day alone, they're pack animals after all. I had a friend once who got rid of her husband's dog after he died because she used to come home from work and find that the dog had messed. When I asked how long it had been left alone, she told me anything between ten and twelve hours, five days a week."

"My God, that's terrible. I hope you tore her off a strip or two."

"I did. Then we parted company. Anyway, getting back on track, what can you tell me about the cottages across the road?"

"Quite a lot. It depends what you're referring to. Are you going to tell me what's going on over there? Those people in white suits are usually from forensics, aren't they? Is there a body over there? Either way, I'm not complaining, the noise of that damn digger was driving me nuts this morning. If that's what we've got to look forward to over the next few months, let's just say I'm glad to see you lot show up and make them stop."

"Yes, you're right in your assumption, they're from forensics and the pathologist's department."

"Good Lord! There are times when you dread being right. How awful. Where was it?"

"We believe it was buried in concrete."

"Intentional then? Jesus, I can't believe what I'm bloody hearing. Never thought I'd see the day. This has always been a trouble-free neighbourhood. Most people got on. There were a few odd neighbours along the line, but they didn't last long, not really."

"Any idea what happened to the cottages?"

"It was terrible. Something that I've feared might happen all my life, a bloody gas explosion. Killed the woman living there at the time."

"Oh no, I wasn't aware of that. What was her name?"

"Edna Davies... I E S at the end. Poor woman, she'd lost her husband a few weeks before. I tried to help her out when I could, but she was often confused. I think she was suffering from dementia but I don't think she was actually diagnosed with it, not as such. Word has it she probably left the gas on and then switched the light on and boom!"

Sally noted down the information. "Did she have any family? Children?"

"No, I think that's why we became good friends in the first place because we had a lot in common."

"How long did she live there?"

"Five years. Before that the Coppells lived there. She was lovely, and he was one of those men you could take or leave. Sometimes really rude, ignoring you in the street, then another day he'd be laughing and joking with you when he was out there cleaning his windows. Like I said, funny bloke."

"Did they have any family?"

"Yes, two girls. A bit reserved, often quiet. Didn't play out in the streets like the other kids. Ran home from school every day, and you didn't lay eyes on them again until the next day."

Sally glanced across the road at the building site. "Did the cottages have gardens?"

"Yes, they were fairly large over there, we definitely drew the short straw on this side of the road."

Again, Sally jotted down the information. "And they lived at number four, is that correct?"

"Yes, sorry, I should have said, that's the cottage that exploded."

"It's okay, I just wanted to ensure the information was accurate. Do you know where the family moved to, the Coppells?"

"Something strange there. Rumour had it that the husband did a moonlight flit and buggered off and left them. I think that's why the woman and the kids left; she had trouble paying the bills on her own."

Sally's interest piqued. "Did you ever see him around again?"

"Nope. Left in the night, never to be seen again."

"What about her or the kids?"

"Funny you should ask that, I was sitting in the lounge one day a few months ago and I noticed a car pull up outside the cottage. A woman got out and peered through the window. Now, I don't mind telling you that she looked familiar. At first, I thought it was Mrs Coppell herself but then I realised it must have been one of the girls instead."

"Interesting. And this was a few months after the explosion had happened?"

"Oh yes, at least two months. Maybe the family heard about it on the local news or something and the girl wanted

31

to pay her final respects to the cottage before the sale went through."

"Sounds logical. Sorry, did you say where they moved to?"

"I think it was pretty local but I couldn't tell you where, I'm sorry."

"No need to apologise, you've been really helpful. I don't suppose you know anything about the other neighbours over there."

"I do. Look, if you can put up with the cat hair lying around, why don't you come in? I have trouble standing for too long, you see."

"I don't mind in the slightest, you'd be shocked at the state of some of the houses we have to visit at times."

"I bet. Come in, dear."

Sally glanced down the road to see if she could gain Lorne's attention, but her partner had her head down, making notes. So, she followed Mrs Lamont through the hallway and into the dated lounge. Sitting on the sofa, curled up on a tartan blanket, was a long-haired cat which opened one of its eyes when she entered the room.

"I take it this is the culprit," Sally said.

"Yes, you sit in my chair, dear, and I'll cosy up next to her."

"Thanks. Now, where were we? Ah, yes, the other neighbours."

Mrs Lamont stroked the cat and rose to her feet once more. "That's right. Let me get my address book, see if that will shed some light on where the previous occupiers are now. You'll have to forgive me, my mind isn't as sharp as it used to be. Hard to imagine me organising meetings galore week in, week out. Never once did I get a ticking off from my boss for letting him down, either. Oh well, at least I'm better off than some folks I know. Too much of this damn dementia around for my liking. Extremely hard to deal with, not only for the person living with the disease but for the family caring for them as well."

"So I've heard. My friend cares for her mother, it's a full-time job, and she never gets a moment to herself. She's refused any kind of help, up till now. However, she broke down the other day, and I forced her to call Social Services, and they've been brilliant so far. So there is definitely help out there if you need it."

"I'm guessing not as much as there should be, though." Book collected, Mrs Lamont returned to her seat. The cat stretched out beside her, and Mrs Lamont stroked her. "Daft cat. I'd be lost without her company. They're more than just pets, aren't they? They're a major part of the family. She's also my best friend. I don't get out much, you see, the body is willing but the legs are far more stubborn now the years are whizzing by. All good things come to an end, I suppose. Nevertheless, I mustn't grumble, although I do, often."

"It must be hard, not being able to do the things you used to do when you were younger, especially if you've led a very active life."

"Oh, it is. Still, at least I have my memories. There are days when I just sit here, whiling away the hours, reliving the good times, when I used to travel around the world with hubby. Not that we got away that much, not compared to others. We ensured we paid off our mortgage first before we started leading a jet-set life." She laughed and smiled as her eyes filled up with tears.

Sally's heart went out to the woman who clearly missed not having her husband around any more. "Do you have any siblings?"

"I had a brother, he was taken from us at a young age. He had a muscle wasting disease where his life expectancy was limited. He sadly died when he was twenty-five."

"I'm sorry to hear that. That's no age at all, is it?"

"No. I did some research on the disease a few months ago, you know, out of interest, and it would appear that medication can be a great asset to sufferers of the disease these days. If only he had been born fifty years later... But then, we can't go through life spouting that, can we?"

"I suppose not." Sally paused, not wishing to make the woman feel pressured into continuing the interview until she was ready.

"Anyway, there's no point going over things that happened a long time ago. Let me try and sort out how I can help you. There were four cottages on that side of the road, I've already told you who lived at number four, haven't I?"

"You have indeed." Sally flipped open her notebook and poised her pen.

"Okay, looking through my address book, I only have the recent owners in here. I'm afraid that's going to have to do."

Sally nodded. "Anything you can give me will be more than welcome. We can work our way back, if we need to."

"Right you are then. At number two was old Ken Smalley. A man in his seventies, I think he moved into sheltered housing. He's always been a very proud man, but having to leave his home the way he did, it absolutely crushed him."

"That's sad." Sally left her seat and got down on one knee to copy the address. "Brilliant. Do you have the other addresses?"

"Yes, let's see now. Ah, here we are; at number six was a middle-aged couple, Rita and Roland Evans. They moved up to near Norwich, to be closer to their daughter and their grandchildren. Lovely couple, always together, they were, barely apart, except when they were working. She worked at the local primary school as a cook, and he worked..., I can't remember, he went to work in a suit every day, if that helps. They adored each other."

Again, Sally made a note of the address Mrs Lamont had

for the couple. She was delighted with the information the kind woman had given her so far and knew it could make a huge difference to the investigation going forward.

"And the final homeowner was Ivy Bailey. I used to be good friends with her, back in the day, but we fell out about ten years ago over something trivial. Saying that, after the explosion, we put our differences aside, and she told me she was moving in with her daughter. They were building an extension for her, it was already on the cards, so they went ahead with the build sooner than they expected. She sent me a letter a few months after, telling me she was having a blast living with her family."

"That's great to hear, and her address now is...?"

She angled the address book so Sally could take down the details once more, then Sally returned to her seat.

"You've been really helpful, I can't thank you enough."

"It's my pleasure. How long has this body been down there, do you know?"

Sally smiled and shook her head. "No, it's far too early to tell."

"What a shame. What an awful thing to discover. I don't have to ask how the workmen are feeling right now, I only have to look at the shock on their faces to know that."

"It's been a devastating find for all concerned. Well, if there's nothing else you think I should know, I'll be off and leave you in peace now."

She tried to get out of her chair, but the effort proved to be too much for her. "I'm sorry, it'll take me a while to recover from my exertions. Can you let yourself out?"

"Stay there, it's fine. Again, I want to thank you for all the information you've given me, I really do appreciate it."

"I like to do my bit to help the police out, always have done, dear. Your job is tough enough as it is, I should imagine."

"It can be, some days. I have a feeling this is going to be one of the easiest cases my team will have to solve, going by what you've told me. I hope that claim doesn't come back to bite me on the backside over the coming weeks or months." Sally laughed.

"I'll look forward to hearing the results on the news, it's bound to be on there soon, isn't it?"

"No doubt. I might even need to put out an appeal if I can't find the previous owners."

"I'm sure that would save a lot of effort on your part."

"I'll see how we go for now. To be honest with you, we don't usually obtain this amount of information in the first few hours of opening up an investigation." She waved her notebook and smiled. "Anyway, I'd better get off. You take good care of yourself, Mrs Lamont."

"I will. Good luck."

Sally let herself out of the cottage and went in search of her partner. Lorne was in the process of completing an interview with the neighbour two doors down. "How did you get on?" Sally asked.

"Nothing worth mentioning so far. You?"

Sally tapped her notebook in her right hand. "I think we've got more than enough to be going on with. Time to get back to the station to sift through what I've been given."

"It's exceptional that you're prepared to skip paying the estate agent and the solicitors a visit."

Sally chewed her lip and wondered if Mrs Lamont's age might work against her with regard to some of the information the woman had given her. "All right, you win. I suppose it's better to be safe than sorry."

CHAPTER 2

Sally decided to call at the solicitors' first. One of the partners, Edward Franks, was only too happy to see them when they showed up without an appointment.

"Take a seat. How can I help you today, Inspector Parker?"

"You can call me Sally. Thank you for agreeing to see us, Mr Franks. This morning we were called to a building site which we believe will now be considered a crime scene."

"You've lost me. What sort of crime?" He sat back in his chair and intertwined his fingers over his round belly that was putting an enormous strain on the buttons of his waistcoat.

"We suspect murder."

"Suspect? Surely, either it's a murder case or it isn't. Why the doubt in your mind?"

"A skeleton was found at a property, and we believe this person was most likely to have been buried in the foundations."

"I see. How awful. And you're here, why?"

"We believe your firm were the solicitors' who dealt with the purchase of the site."

"Oh, right. Perhaps, we've dealt with a couple of cases of that ilk recently. Do you know who bought the site?"

"A Kevin Galen, he's the builder. I should have asked if he purchased the land under a company name."

"You're in luck, I happen to know Kevin very well. He's purchased several properties through us over the past ten years or so. Let me guess, are you talking about the site out at Watton?"

"That's correct."

"I only suggested that one because that's his most recent acquisition and I'm aware that he was about to begin construction on it soon. Damn, finding remains on the site is only going to set the build back, isn't it?"

"That's usually what it amounts to. I'll be honest with you, before we left the site, my partner and I carried out house-to-house enquiries, and we acquired a fair amount of information about the occupants of the cottages concerned from one of the neighbours across the road. What I am hoping for was that if we can compare notes, if you like?"

"Compare notes? You mean you want me to supply you with the names and addresses of the owners of the cottages that were destroyed in the explosion?"

"Yes. Sorry for going around in circles to get there."

"Let's not do that in the future, just come right out and say it."

Sally's cheeks heated up. "Sorry, I'll be sure to do that. There were a couple of addresses that Mrs Lamont, the neighbour who shared the details with us, wasn't too sure about."

"Wait, why are you interested in speaking to the previous owners? Correction, what I should have said was the *most recent* owners. Do you know how long the body has been buried on site?"

"No, everything is up in the air regarding that just now."

"I see. I'm not saying I won't give you the addresses. Of course, I'm going to need a warrant for you to obtain them due to the new regulations put in place, the General Data Protection Regulation, however, my query would be, if the remains you discovered turn out to be over twenty years old and the previous owners have only lived at the cottage for say, ten years."

"I understand. I'd rather not go down the warrant route, I'm sure my team will come up with the goods." *Can't stand dealing with a jobsworth, it won't work, I'm confident my team will come up trumps, and soon. Maybe I should bear you in mind as a suspect, now there's a thought!*

"Do you know how the victim died?"

"Again, nothing I can reveal on that front either. Thank you for seeing us."

The three of them rose from their seats. Sally's heart sank as she walked towards the door. They shook hands with Mr Franks and left the office.

Outside, on the way to the car, Sally said, "And bang, just like that, our day just went from good to bad."

"Eh? How do you make that one out?"

"I thought we were on a roll, having access to all this information so early on, and then the rug is pulled from under our feet."

"You're being a bit melodramatic about all this, Sal. Just put this setback aside until the team find the addresses and, in the meantime, we can go through the details we've been given." Lorne pointed across the road. "Umm... would it be worth making a stop at the estate agent's, just in case?"

"Well, that's a stroke of luck. Yep, let's try a different tack this time and see where that gets us."

"We can try," Lorne agreed.

They crossed the road and entered the estate agent's office. A man and a woman were sitting behind the desks.

The man was dealing with a young couple obviously looking to either buy or rent one of the properties the agency had to offer.

The female agent approached them. "Hello, I'm Jen, how can I help you today?"

Sally showed her ID. "I'm DI Sally Parker, and this is my partner, DS Lorne Warner. Is it possible to speak to the person in charge?"

"That's me. I'm the manager, for my sins. The police, this has to be a first, I've never had a visit from the police before. What's it concerning?"

"Is there somewhere private we can talk? This is a little too public for what I have to say."

"Blimey, that doesn't sound good. Yes, okay, there's a staffroom out the back, will that do?"

"I'm sure that will be fine."

She led the way through the desks, her associate and his clients all having a nose as they walked past. Once they had relocated to the tiny staffroom, Jen offered them a seat, but neither Sally nor Lorne accepted one.

"We're fine, hopefully this won't take us long."

"Okay, have either I or my colleague done something illegal? Is that why you're here?"

Sally raised her hand. "Oh, no, I'm sorry if that's how it came across. We're investigating a crime scene and could do with some assistance from you."

"Me? May I ask in what respect? What sort of crime scene?"

"The remains of a body were found at a construction site this morning, and we need to trace the previous owners of the properties."

"Oh heck. Was the body buried under a patio or something?"

"We're not sure of the ins and outs at present. We were

told that you sold the properties to a Kevin Galen a few months ago."

"Yes, I remember. He was going to apply for planning permission to erect a block of flats which I doubt would go down well with the locals."

"I'm not sure whether that was the case or not. The construction work began today, and a few hours later the men had to down tools after making the discovery."

"How long has the body been there?" Jen collapsed into one of the chairs and placed her head in her hands.

"We can't be certain of the timescale as yet. The pathologist and her team are still at the site, collecting evidence."

"But you're here asking for the previous owners' details, why? You think one of them bumped someone off and buried them at one of the properties?"

Sally sighed and also sank into one of the available chairs. "It's something that we seriously need to consider."

"Christ, how horrendous. Do you think the explosion took place to cover up the crime?"

Sally cocked an eyebrow. Her suspicions hadn't even gone down that particular route yet. "Possibly, we won't know until we start interviewing the people who lived there. That's where you come in. Can you give us the addresses of the last known residents?" *Best to ask in case the team miss anything crucial.*

"Yes, of course. If we don't have where they're living now, we'll have where they were staying after the explosion occurred, if that makes sense. My goodness, this is hard to process, isn't it? I never thought I'd ever have to deal with the police after selling a property. It has to be a first. Is there anything else you need to know while I'm at it?"

"Contact numbers for the sellers would be great, too." Sally intentionally omitted revealing to the young woman that she already had the addresses to hand, just in case they turned out to be fake for some reason. It wouldn't be the first time they had come across a similar situation in the past.

Jen left the room and returned five minutes later with a cluster of files in her arms. "I managed to find them all, sorry for the delay."

"Don't be. This looks promising."

Lorne opened her notebook and primed her pen ready.

"There were four properties." She gave them the same details Mrs Lamont had furnished Sally with earlier. The only minor difference was in Mr Smalley's details, the man who lived at number two. His address turned out to be a temporary one because he'd stayed with his daughter for a couple of months until he got to the top of the waiting list.

"You've been extremely helpful, we really appreciate it."

"My pleasure. Is there anything else you need?" Jen smiled.

"I think that's all for now unless you've had a hand in selling the properties previously?"

"I can certainly have a look for you. I'll check what details we have on the system, it might be easier than going through the files in person."

"You're too kind. Shall we stay here?"

"It's up to you. Clive's finished with the customers he was dealing with now, so it's all clear out there for a while. Maybe he'll be able to add something extra; he's the type to never forget a name."

"Might be worth having a chat with him in that case, thanks," Sally agreed.

They headed back to the main office, and Jen made the introductions and invited Sally and Lorne to take a seat.

Sally sat opposite Clive who was in his mid-to-late thirties. "Sorry for the inconvenience we're causing."

He waved her suggestion away. "Nonsense, it's all good. It's nice to have a breather between customers, although saying that, I'm going to have to leave in about fifteen minutes as I have a viewing. It's not far, though."

"We won't hold you up, I promise."

Jen gave him the lowdown on the information she was searching for on the system. "Oh heck, now you're testing me. All the owners had lived at their respective properties for around ten to fifteen years. I started here around twelve years ago, so I'm not going to be any help on that front, I'm afraid."

"It's fine. I know we were probably expecting too much asking in the first place."

Jen glanced their way. "Yeah, I'm not having much luck with the system either. Sorry about that."

"Don't be. The information you've given us so far will help get the investigation underway."

Sally bid them both farewell, and she and Lorne left the building.

"At least you've got the phone numbers for a few people. We can start making the relevant calls to get the investigation underway once we're back at the station," Lorne said on the way back to the car.

"Yeah, we can start putting a plan into action, ready to go ahead with things in the morning."

"Maybe by then we'll know more about the crime scene and the victim."

"Here's hoping. Thank God we've got Jack's leaving do to occupy our minds this evening. It was great seeing him today. I never expected to tear up the way I did."

"It's hard saying goodbye to a partner you've been with for what? Ten or twelve years?"

"About that. I can't tell you off the top of my head, you know as well as I do how quickly time flies. It's scary, isn't it?"

They both got in the car.

"Tell me about it. It only seems like five minutes ago when Charlie was a tearaway of a teenager. Now look at her, a serving police officer with a couple of years' service under her belt already."

"Yeah, that's scary all right. How are you feeling? Have you got your menopause symptoms under control now?"

"I seem to have, only time will tell. The doctor said she might have to make a few tweaks somewhere along the line in the future if anything changes."

"That's great news. I must say, I've seen an improvement in your day-to-day moods."

Lorne sat forward and faced her. "What? Was I really that bad?"

"Let's just say you had your moments."

"Why didn't you say something?"

Sally placed a hand over her heart. "In all honesty, I thought you and Tony were having marital problems and I didn't want to interfere, thought you would open up to me sooner or later."

Lorne settled into her seat once more and clunked her seat belt in place. "Never, not in a million years. I wouldn't wish what I've been going through lately on anyone. Unless you've been through the menopause, no one can really understand."

"That's why you should have opened up to me. A problem shared and all that crap."

BACK AT THE STATION, Sally spent the next ten minutes bringing the team up to date on what had occurred while they were out. She sipped at her now lukewarm coffee. "So we need to get on the phones and start calling some of these people, if they're still with us."

"What about Coppell?" Lorne asked. "Want me to see if the family ever registered him as missing?"

"Good idea. Let's work with the information we have to hand and see if we can expand on that. I'll be in my office. Good luck, guys, I know you won't let me down." Sally marched into her office, sat at her desk and let out a large sigh. She glanced at her watch. It was four-thirty already, no wonder she was beginning to feel tired. She groaned inwardly at the thought of having to pin a smile on her face at Jack's party. *A bit of notice might have been good, Jack. Never mind, I hope we can give him the send-off he deserves, later.*

Sally immersed herself in the pile of paperwork littering her desk that she'd been sifting her way through before the news had broken about the remains being discovered. Lorne knocked on the door about ten minutes later.

"Sorry to disturb you, I have a small update for you."

Sally beckoned her. "Come in, sit down."

"I've managed to track down Ken Smalley who lived at number two and arranged to pay him a visit in the morning at ten."

"That's excellent news. You didn't tell him why, did you?"

"No, I just said we had a query or two about the site, that's all."

"And he accepted that?"

"He appeared to. Also, Joanna has managed to trace Mrs Bailey from number eight. She's willing to see us tomorrow as well."

"This gets better and better. What about the other two cottages?"

"We're still trying."

"Also, I rang Missing Persons, and they told us that Paul Coppell had never been registered as a missper with them."

Stroking her chin between her thumb and forefinger, Sally said, "How strange, I wonder why that was."

"Maybe the marriage wasn't all it was cracked up to be and the wife was relieved when he walked out."

"I don't suppose you've had time to carry out a national search on him, have you?"

Lorne cocked an eyebrow. "In ten minutes?"

"All right, I was only asking because I know how efficient you are."

"That's next on my agenda. You haven't forgotten we're supposed to be meeting Jack over the road at six, have you?"

"As if I would. I was sitting here thinking he could have given us a bit more notice, but I wouldn't let him down, not intentionally. We needn't stay long, need we?"

"That's what I was thinking, on both counts. If you want a proper drink tonight, I can drive you home and pick you up in the morning."

"The way I'm feeling right now, don't tempt me. I could do with a good session, but maybe we should leave that for the weekend instead. You and Tony can come round for a barbecue, how does that sound?"

"Only if the weather stays fine. I think it's supposed to be a bit hit and miss at the weekend."

"Typical. Anyway, I'm going to politely ask you to piss off and let me finish tackling this lot. Hopefully I can clear most of it now, leaving us free to get on with the investigation first thing in the morning."

"Until more lands on your desk overnight."

Sally screwed her nose up. "I was trying not to think about that. Get out of here and allow me to crack on."

"Your wish is my command, oh powerful one."

Sally screwed up a sheet of paper and aimed it at her partner who scooted out of the room, anticipating the move.

. . .

JACK WAS WAITING for them when they entered the pub. His head was bowed, and he was staring into his pint of orange juice. Sally suspected he was probably wishing it was a pint of bitter instead.

She slapped him on the back. "How's it diddling, partner?"

"Christ, you scared the shit out of me." He turned to face them all and beamed. "And there was me thinking you weren't going to show up."

Sally tutted. "We're only five minutes late, you know what the end of a shift routine can be like."

He frowned. "Two seconds to turn off the computers and tidy your desk."

Sally chuckled. "Maybe you did that when you worked with us, matey. Most of us prefer to give as much attention to the end of the day as we do at the beginning."

Jack groaned. "Whatever. You're here, finally. What's everyone having? The first round is on me."

The team placed their orders with him and then congregated around the large table towards the back of the public bar.

"I'll bring them over," Jack shouted, as if he had an option.

Lorne leaned in and whispered to Sally, "He seems relieved we've shown up."

"I thought the same. Bless him."

Jack joined them with a tray of drinks a little while later and distributed them to the team. They all raised a glass, and it was down to Sally to say a few words in the way of a toast.

"To Jack. God help Donna having to contend with his mood swings in the years ahead."

Jack's mouth hung open. Everyone else cheered and knocked back their drinks.

"And I thought I could count on you lot as friends." He took a sip of his orange juice and winced.

Sally threw an arm around his shoulder. "Imagine it's a pint of beer and neck it."

"Not likely, this has to last me all evening, not sure I could stomach more than this one."

"Hey, where is Donna? I thought she was coming tonight."

"No, she had a prior engagement that she couldn't get out of."

"Gone to bingo, has she, mate?" Jordan joked.

"As it happens, yes."

The group all roared again.

The banter continued back and forth between them for the next couple of hours. Sally had lots to reveal about the antics Jack had got up to, and the others were only too eager to hear.

"Remember that time I had to save the day when that bloke over in Hethersett said he wanted to string you up?" Jack said.

Sally frowned and shook her head. "Can't say I do. What about him?"

"I held back from jumping to your defence only for him to end up flat on his back ten seconds later. You wiped the floor with him, literally."

"One of many, eh, Jack? We've had some good times over the years, you and me. Far too many incidents to mention where I lost my temper with you for being a plonker."

"Yeah, probably. Most of the time I acted like an idiot just to wind you up."

"Bollocks!" Sally replied. "You think I didn't know when you were being serious? You're all too easy to read, mate."

"Whatever. You keep telling yourself that, Sally. Anyway, enough about me, how's my replacement settling into her new role?"

Lorne turned to Sally and asked, "Yes, how am I settling in?"

Sally held her hand up and waved it from side to side. "Fair to middling. She's got more brains than my previous partner."

"Bloody hell. I've heard it all now," Jack complained.

"Hey, going over past experiences, here's one I'm sure you'd rather I didn't air in public."

As if he knew what was coming next, Jack hid his face with his hand and peered through his fingers. "No, you can't. You wouldn't dare... shit, why did I have to say that?"

Sally chuckled. "I'm definitely going to tell them now, you know the dare word is like a red rag to a bull. There was this one occasion when we were interviewing this young woman who clearly had the hots for our have-a-go hero here. He was sat there, sucking up all the attention until the body builder boyfriend came into the room and found this girl, April, I think she was called, draped all over Jack."

"Oh shit, what happened?" Joanna asked.

"I've never seen Jack move so fast in all my life. He unwrapped the woman's arm from round his neck and jumped off the sofa. I was in a chair by the door. This bloke let out a growl and crossed the room towards Jack. I had to intervene and stretched out a leg to trip the bloke up. I then slapped my handcuffs on him before he realised what the hell was going on. In the meantime, April had raced across the room to check if Jack was all right. Laughable, it was, like a scene out of one of those slapstick comedies that used to be shoved down our necks years ago."

"You do talk a lot of rot at times," Jack objected. "The woman was upset so I was comforting her, only because Miss Standoffish, with no sympathy running through her bones over here, thought this girl was beneath her."

Sally's head jutted forward. "What the fuck are you on about, man? As if I'd do something like that, it's not in my nature. Anyway, admit it, you were relieved when I felled the mighty oak of a boyfriend before he had a chance to put his hands on you."

"Never in a million years. I had it all in hand."

"Of course you did. It took me half an hour to calm the goon down. I ordered you to sit in the car before I removed the cuffs. Any other officer would have remained there and offered me some support. Not you, you couldn't get out of the house quickly enough. Sod what was likely to happen to me in the process."

"Another lie. I tweaked my back in my haste to get away from the young woman and felt it would be better if I waited outside in the car for you."

"What happened to the boyfriend? I bet he was livid having the cuffs slapped on him," Lorne asked, her gaze shifting quickly between Sally and Jack.

"He was. I managed to work my magic on him and calmed the situation down. Told him what would happen if he decided to take things further. He backed down but issued a warning that I should pass on to Jack."

"Which was?" Jordan asked.

"He told him to stay clear of the gym they both used or suffer the consequences."

"Wow, so you knew him then?" Lorne asked Jack.

His eyes widened, and he held his palms up. "What the fuck? This is the first I'm hearing about this."

The team laughed.

"So you continued to use the gym?" Jordan asked.

"Yeah, why wouldn't I? I didn't know the guy from Adam." He faced Sally and said, "Thanks for putting my life at risk, I really appreciate it."

Sally grinned. "The pleasure was all mine, partner. Right, one more round, and then I'm going to have to call it a day."

Lorne helped Sally to collect the drinks from the bar.

"He seems on a downer. Do you think it's because this'll

be his last trip to the pub with all of us or because Donna preferred to go elsewhere this evening?" Lorne asked.

Sally discreetly peered over her shoulder at Jack. "The former. I don't think it's hit him just what he's about to give up, until now."

"Poor bloke. I know he rebelled at first when you switched over to being a cold case team but I think deep down he grew to enjoy it, even if he never openly came out and admitted it to you."

"I think you're right. Maybe he sees this as just another failure in his chequered past. He was forced to quit the army through the injuries he sustained whilst on tour, and now it's happened all over again."

"Yeah, possibly. I think I would feel a failure confronted with that truth as well. I suppose he could always have a word with Tony."

Sally's eyes widened. "Bugger, I never thought about that. I think it would be an excellent suggestion. Maybe you should run it past Tony first, what do you think?"

"He wouldn't mind. He's over it. Leaving MI6 was a blessing in disguise all those years ago because of the injury he sustained. Yes, he gets the odd twinge in his leg now and again, but it's nothing to what he had to contend with when he first came back from that godawful place. I still cringe when I hear Afghanistan mentioned on the news. He doesn't. Nothing fazes him. He's such a brave man, the bravest man I've ever known. Why don't we invite Jack and Donna to the barbecue at the weekend? I could have a word with Tony, see if he'd be willing to have a quiet word in Jack's ear while we distract Donna."

Sally high-fived Lorne. "What an excellent idea. Don't mention anything in front of the others, I'll see if I can catch him alone later. If not, I'll give him a call tomorrow."

"That'll be twenty-four ninety, thanks," the barman said.

"Holy crap. I wasn't planning to pay the pub's rent for the month, I only wanted to buy a round for my friends."

Lorne laughed. "I'll get it if you're short."

"I'm not, I'm my usual height," Sally was quick to retort.

"I've got other customers waiting," the barman said, his lack of humour clear to see.

Sally rolled her eyes, opened her purse and removed her debit card. "Thank God payday is just around the corner."

"Amen to that," Lorne replied. "It's been an extra-busy month on the outgoing side at the kennels."

"Shit, sorry, me and my big mouth. I can be so selfish at times. If you ever need a hand financially, I can help out now and again."

Lorne sighed. "Behave, we're fine. Now forget I mentioned it. Come on, they'll be wondering where we've got to."

"We'll drink this and go, okay?" Sally noticed the clock above the bar. It was already seven-thirty.

"Yep, time's marching on sure enough."

IN THE END, Sally called time on the evening at eight-fifteen. Most of the group remained behind, but she and Lorne made their way towards the car park. Jack went with them, just to ensure they made it to the car safely.

"Our hero, what are we going to do without having you around to watch over us?" Sally said in a breathless tone.

"Get out of here, you wind-up merchant. I wanted to thank you both for coming this evening, it's meant the world to me. You've all been brilliant. I expected you to only stay for one round and shoot off."

Sally playfully slapped his arm. "When are you going to realise how much you mean to us, big man?"

His cheeks turned crimson. "That's excellent. You guys

mean a lot to me, too. You're more like family than work colleagues, or should I say, former work colleagues. That's going to be the strangest part, considering you all as former colleagues."

"Time's a great healer, Jack. Anyway, talking of time, we're going to have to make a move. Hey, we're having a barbecue on Saturday, there will only be the four of us there, we'd love for you and Donna to join us. What say you?"

The grin that appeared lit up his face. "Are you kidding me? We'd be honoured. What time do you want us there? Donna's bound to ask, do you need us to bring anything? Apart from the usual bottle of wine, that is."

"No, we'll have it all covered. I'll give you a ring later on in the week to make sure we're still on track, okay?" She hugged him tightly and kissed him on the cheek.

"Aww… thanks, Sal, not just for coming tonight but for everything. Being there when Donna needed you most after the accident. For being the best partner and boss anyone could ever wish to have. For *everything*." Tears welled up, and he brushed them away with the back of his hand. "I swore I wasn't going to do this."

"You big softie. You'll always be a huge part of my life. Don't be a stranger, Jack. I mean it. If ever you or Donna need anything, don't hesitate to get in touch, okay?"

His Adam's apple bobbed up and down, and he nodded, unable to speak.

"Go on, go back to the others, that's an order."

He hugged Sally and then Lorne. "I know you won't let her down, Lorne. I'm glad she tempted you out of retirement, you two are going to be a force to be reckoned with, there's no doubt in my mind about that."

It was Lorne's turn to tear up. "Thanks, Jack. Hey, like Sally said, don't be a stranger. Let us know how you're doing, often, got that?"

"Yeah, thanks again, both of you. A man couldn't wish or hope for better friends. I'm going now, before I make a complete and utter fool out of myself."

They shared a final group hug, and then Sally and Lorne got into Lorne's car. Jack waved them off.

"Bless him, he's still there," Lorne said as they left the car park.

"He's a good 'un. I can't help feeling guilty about the way I've treated him over the years. He wasn't always the easiest of partners to get along with at times, especially during the transition. He drove me to distraction during that period."

Lorne reached over and squeezed her thigh and stated quietly, "At least he's still around, that's what you need to cling on to, love. Times move on but you guys will always remain friends, I guarantee it."

Sally sniffled. "You're right, as usual. God, I wish I hadn't had that final drink, my head is swimming."

"Good job I offered to drive you home then. Hey, it's okay to let your hair down now and again, and it was for an excellent cause."

Sally tipped her head back and closed her eyes for a moment or two. Lorne woke her up when she drew onto the gravelled drive outside her home. "Blimey, that's a first, me drifting off like that. How rude of me."

"Think nothing of it. I enjoyed the peace and quiet for a change."

"Charming. I take it you don't want to hang around for another?" Sally surprised herself by slurring.

"No, Tony will be wanting his tea, we both know how useless he is in the kitchen."

"He might surprise you, have dinner waiting on the table for you."

"Surprise? I'd be absolutely shocked if ever that were to

happen. See you in the morning; what time shall I pick you up?"

"About eight-thirty, that's not too wirly for you, is it?"

Lorne smiled. "I was about to suggest the same. That'll give me time to try ringing the others on my list before we head off to visit Smalley."

"You're a good egg, Lorne. Well organised and always willing to do your bit for the team. A twue warrior, the Force is wucky to have you back."

"Get out of here, you're getting too slushy with the praise now. Enjoy the rest of your evening, if you last that long."

"I might have a bath and go straight to bed."

"I think by the look of Simon wearing his apron, he's got other plans in mind."

Sally's gaze shifted to the front door of the manor house she shared with her wonderful husband. "You could be right. In that case, I'm prepared to suffer. As long as he doesn't expect me to cook, everything is fine and dandy with me." She opened the door and tipped out of the car. "Oops, lost my footing for a moment there."

"God help Simon this evening. See you soon."

Sally waved, and Lorne drew away.

Sally turned towards the house only to bump into Simon. "Oh dear, I didn't see you there."

"That much was evident. I take it you had a good evening."

"We did. We gave him the send-off he deserved."

"That's great to hear. Hungry? I've made an authentic lasagne."

Sally resisted the urge to retch. "Sounds lovely, just a little perhaps. It's been a long day, and I'm a bit tired."

"I can always save it for tomorrow and cook you an omelette instead."

"Sounds much better, you're a sweetheart. What would I do without you?" she slurred.

"I'm guessing that you'd starve most days. Let's get you inside."

"I have to take Dex for a walk first."

"You mean a stagger, judging by the way you're walking. How many have you had?"

"One or two, maybe three, I lost count. It was worth it, though. Jack was so pleased we showwwed up tonight. He's coming for a barbecue at the weekend, he and Donna, Lorne and Tony. That's all right, isn't it, dahhhling?"

"We'll discuss it in the morning, when you're sober."

"Okay." She lifted her head and smiled up at him. "I wuve you so much."

"I love you, too. And don't worry about Dex, I took him for a long walk earlier, down by the river."

"You're the bestest. My two boys out on a jolly together, how wunderrrful..."

Simon clung tighter to her waist and guided her up the front steps to the fabulous grand entrance. He took her into the kitchen and pulled out a chair then made himself busy, preparing ingredients for the omelette. Dex came and sat beside her, his head tilting from side to side as if trying to work out what was wrong with her.

"Hello, boy. Have you had a good day?" She bent to kiss the tip of his nose, but he turned away from her and returned to his basket. "Hey, what's wrong with you? He refused to give me a kiss," she complained.

Simon laughed. "I might do the same when we get upstairs."

"I'm not that bad... am I?" She caught sight of herself in the mirror above the dresser on the wall in front of her and screwed up her nose. "Yeah, I am. Bugger, I'm sowwy."

Simon completed the omelette and placed it in front of

her five minutes later. She took a mouthful, and her stomach rejected it. "I'm sowwy," she repeated and ran across the room to throw up in the sink.

"Come on, you. Time for bed," Simon said, not even flinching.

"I might need to stop off in the bathroom first."

CHAPTER 3

*L*orne collected her the following morning at eight-thirty on the dot. Sally's head was still thick and muggy, and her stomach wasn't faring much better either.

"Jesus, you look rough."

"I reckon they must have been serving dodgy vodka at the pub last night. I've spent more time in the bathroom than in the bedroom."

"I bet that went down well with Simon."

"He's been a true gent about it. He even offered to fetch me the spare quilt and pillow so I could sleep in the bath."

Lorne laughed. "Now that's a thoughtful man."

"Stop it! I feel so bad. I can't remember the last time I got this drunk. I was all right in the pub. It was when the fresh air hit me, that's when the damage was done."

"If you insist. Are you going to be all right to interview people today?"

"A litre or two of coffee should do the trick. If it doesn't, then you'll have to take the lead. I'm so glad I cleared my desk yesterday, I couldn't have coped with dealing with that crap today."

"Maybe you should consider popping a couple of pills if you feel that bad. Or even having a day off."

"Not going to happen, I've never had a day off because of the demon drink before and don't intend to start now. I'll be fine soon. All right if I have the window open?"

"Of course."

Once they reached the station, Sally stopped off at the ladies' toilets and took one look at her dreadful appearance in the mirror. Her heart sank. "Why do it to yourself?" she asked her reflection.

She splashed her face with water, dried it on a couple of paper towels and threw them in the bin. Back in the incident room, the rest of the team seemed a little subdued, all except Lorne, who had wisely been on the orange juice with Jack.

"I think I'll follow your example in the future and stick with the OJs," Sally said, perching on the desk beside her partner.

"Seems an excellent idea to me. What time do you want to leave?"

"How long is it going to take us to get there?"

"Fifteen minutes tops."

"We'll head out at about nine-forty then. I'll be in my office, hunting through my drawers for some stomach settlers."

Lorne opened the drawer to her right and removed a packet of Rennies. "Here you go."

"You never cease to amaze me, you're always coming to my rescue."

"Hardly."

Sally collected a cup of water on the way to her office and settled down behind her desk just as her landline rang. She quickly flicked out a couple of Rennies and put them on her desk ready to take after she'd dealt with the call. "Hello, DI Sally Parker, how may I help?"

"Hello DI Parker, this is Lyn Porter. DCI Green would like to see you if you have a moment."

"Of course. I have to go out shortly. I'll pop along now, if that's okay?"

"See you soon. Thank you."

Sally hung up, groaned, placed the chewable tablets in her mouth and set off. "I've been summoned," she told Lorne as she passed.

"Oops, I hope you're up to it."

"I will be soon. See you later. You have my permission to come and rescue me if I'm not back within thirty minutes."

Lorne giggled. "Roger that."

DCI Green was a tough, no-nonsense type of man. From day one and at the beginning of their working relationship, he'd made a point of laying down the law. Telling her in no uncertain terms what he expected from her as his second-in-command. So far, their relationship had been a reasonable one but had still had its moments when Sally had pushed him too far.

She walked into his secretary's office. "Hi, Lyn."

"Good morning, Inspector Parker. Nice morning out there."

"It is, too nice to be stuck inside today."

"I thought the same whilst taking my dog out first thing. Roll on retirement."

"That's years off yet, surely, isn't it?"

"Two years, and I'm counting down the days."

"Goodness me, I... no, I won't say it."

Lyn smiled. "You didn't realise I was that old, eh?" She fluffed up her hair. "It's out of a bottle—the only fake thing about me, I hasten to add."

Sally plucked a couple of grey hairs at her temple. "I think I'll have to resort to doing that soon enough. Is he in?"

"Yes, go through, he's expecting you."

"Should I be concerned?"

"I don't think so. I'm sure you'll find out soon enough."

Sally cringed and knocked on Green's door. He bellowed for her to enter, so she opened the door and walked in.

"Good morning, sir. You wanted to see me?" She made sure she kept her tone light and breezy, disguising how she truly felt.

"Ah, yes, come in and sit down, Inspector Parker."

Sally did as instructed, thankful her legs felt strong enough to carry her this morning, unlike the previous evening when Simon had met her at the front door.

"I wanted to know what's going on with this new investigation you're working on." He sat upright, his gaze piercing her soul.

"We only started working on it yesterday, sir. It's far too early to say how it's going so far."

"Do you know who the victim is?"

"No. The pathologist hasn't given me her report yet. I'm hoping that will appear sometime today."

"Chase it up. Keep on top of her."

"I will, not that she needs it. She's more than capable of doing her job correctly from what I've seen so far."

"She has exceptional shoes to fill, doesn't she?"

"And I think she's going to fill them just fine, given time. Why the interest in this case, sir?"

"I'm interested in every case my teams work on, Inspector, you should know that by now. Tell me what you've learned so far."

"We showed up at a building site yesterday to find human remains. The pathologist has given us a rough idea that we're probably dealing with a male victim, with an added caveat she wouldn't be able to confirm if that was true until the PM had been carried out."

"I see. So, what's your next step?"

"We've managed to track down a few of the previous owners of the cottages that were knocked down. DS Warner and I are due to visit a couple of them this morning."

"Do we know where the body was buried?"

"No, still waiting for the assessment from the tech team. To me, where it was discovered was mid-row, so the middle two cottages would be my best guess."

"And does the pathologist know how long the body has been buried?"

"Again, I'm awaiting confirmation."

He sighed and leaned back. "Well, well, well, you do seem to have a puzzling investigation ahead of you, don't you?"

"If nothing else, my team and I appreciate a challenge, and I sense this one is going to be one marked with a capital C."

"Talking of your team, would it be wrong of me to ask how your new partner is getting on?"

"Pretty much the way I thought she would. She's never let me down yet, nor is she likely to."

"I know you go back years, I have faith in the pair of you. However, a word of advice for you, you should never allow your friendship to cloud your judgement about her work."

Sally frowned and inclined her head. "Is something on your mind, sir? Has Lorne spoken out of turn or stepped on anyone's toes since she's been here?"

He sat forward and held her gaze for a long time before he eventually answered, "I'm just saying... well, I suppose... I don't really know how to put this without it coming across as..."

Sally was pissed off with his stuttering and gestured for him to spit out what was on the tip of his tongue then mentally kicked herself in case Green perceived her as being rude.

"I'm getting there. It's just that a few of the DCIs and I were discussing all the shit that's going on down in London, in the Met and..."

Sally wagged her finger like a metronome. "No way. I'm not about to sit here and have you believe that Lorne had anything to do with that shit. What the fuck...? I apologise for the use of my language, sir, but really? You truly believe that she...?" It was her turn to be lost for words.

"No, not entirely, but the conversation definitely made me sit up and think."

Sally inhaled a couple of calming breaths, which in turn gave her enough thinking time to challenge him. "Can I be the one to point out that the problems surrounding the Met are mostly misogynistic, or had that fact escaped your notice?"

His gaze darted to the left then the right and eventually fell to the desk. "Umm... perhaps. But, as you well know, that wasn't the only problem to be highlighted in the Met. It's just, what with her coming here, to a sleepy backwater if you will... I'm not making this easy, for either of us, am I?"

"No, sir. I'm sorry, but if you had serious doubts about Lorne, why on earth did you promote her in the first place?"

"I haven't... not really. As I said, a few of us were talking and it got me thinking, that's all."

"I'm sorry, I don't tend to listen to idle gossip, I've always tried to make up my own mind about people, and funnily enough, I thought you were cut from the same cloth."

His gaze met hers, and his eyes narrowed. "I think we'd better end this conversation here before one of us says something that we're likely to regret."

"I wholeheartedly agree. If Lorne had done something wrong, making you question her promotion, I could and would, probably understand where you are coming from, but to sink this low without a genuine reason... is well and truly beyond me. Sorry for being brutally honest, sir, but that about sums it up. I can vouch for Lorne's professionalism without hesitation and would stake my pension on her always putting the Force first. Nothing has changed in that respect." Anger mounted. Sally fidgeted in her seat, her head clearing enough for her to go on an all-out attack to preserve her best friend's reputation. "Actually, in Lorne's defence, she was one of the women in the Met who struggled daily to change so many procedures down there. Her fight to arm every police officer working the streets of London gained admiration for her far and wide."

He held his head in shame and muttered, "I didn't know that. Maybe I should spend more of my time researching the people on my team rather than listening to a bunch of middle-aged men talking out of their arses."

His gaze met Sally's once more, and she couldn't help but smile.

"I couldn't have put it better myself. Now, if there's nothing else, sir, I'd like to get on with solving this investigation ASAP."

"We're through here. I'm sorry that I ever raised the subject, but I'll tell you this, Inspector..."

"What's that, sir?"

"You've just proved what a fantastic inspector you are, defending a member of your team with the courage of a lioness."

"Sorry, did I come across too fierce?"

"Yes, and yet no. The right balance. You're a force to be reckoned with when you're adamant about something, I'll give you that."

"Thank you, sir, I will only stick up for my team if they're in the right, though, so you needn't think otherwise."

"Good to know. Now, get out of this office and go in search of the truth behind your mystery discovery. As always, keep me informed about how the investigation is progressing throughout. I have to admit, I'm more than a little intrigued by this one."

"Me, too, although there's a fine line between intrigue and frustration. I'm going to make sure the frustration is kept to a minimum throughout."

"I'm sure you'll succeed, you always do."

Sally smiled and left the room. She breathed a sigh of relief and leaned against the door once it was closed behind her.

"Everything all right, Inspector Parker?" Lyn asked, concern etched into her features.

"Yes, I'm fine. It was one of those meetings that could have veered off course, however, you'll be pleased to know, I survived it and so did a member of my team."

Lyn frowned and nodded. "That's excellent news, I think."

Sally giggled and pushed herself away from the door. "Must fly, I have people I need to interview this morning."

"Good luck with your investigation, Inspector."

Sally waved and left the office. She stopped off at the ladies' before collecting Lorne from the incident room. Peering into the mirror, she was relieved to see she appeared far brighter than she had when she'd first arrived. Had she visited the chief before she'd had a chance to finish her coffee, she feared the outcome of their meeting would have been somewhat different.

"AREN'T you going to tell me how your meeting with DCI Green went, or shouldn't I ask?" Lorne prompted her during the journey to visit their first interviewee.

"Same old, same old. He wanted to know what was going on with the new case."

"Blimey, we've only been on it a day. He's keen."

"That's something you'll need to get used to if there's ever a time that you need to stand in for me. He's always eager to keep on top of the investigation, even if there's very little to go on."

"Thanks for the warning, not that it's likely to happen... me standing in for you."

"What? Of course it will, at some point. I'm entitled to time off, just like everyone else is at the station."

"Ah, yes, of course, I was forgetting about holiday times, silly me. What was his take on the case?"

"He turned out to be as perplexed as we are right now. Still, hopefully that will change over the next few hours."

Lorne held up her crossed fingers. "I feel good about today. I've not felt this optimistic about an investigation in a long time."

Sally cocked an eyebrow. "Let's hope you don't live to regret those words at the end of our shift."

Lorne crossed her legs and eyes, and they both laughed.

"Here's hoping. You seem brighter than when I picked you up this morning."

"The shock of being summoned by the DCI, I suppose." Sally briefly glanced at the satnav on the dashboard. "Another five minutes and we'll be there. Can you use the time to jot down a few details we need to cover, you know, just in case I slip up and forget something important?"

"Of course. Not that you will. You're on the ball most of the time."

"Yeah, but I haven't had an unnerving visit with the DCI first thing in a while."

"Ah, right, I'm with you. I'm on it."

. . .

A FEW MINUTES LATER, Sally pulled into the gated community of sheltered housing apartments. She parked close to the entrance in the nearest available spot. They entered the building and flashed their IDs to the receptionist on duty behind the wooden counter positioned in the centre of the large, bright and airy foyer. There was a vending machine full of snacks and chocolates in the far corner and a seating area with magazines spread out in a fan on the low table beside half a dozen chairs.

"Oh, yes. You've come to see Mr Smalley. He informed us you were on your way to see him. I'll get someone to show you up to his room; it's at the far end on the top floor but down a hallway that's tucked away and difficult to find."

"If you wouldn't mind, that would be very kind of you."

She picked up a phone and summoned a man called Keith. He swiftly arrived and led them through the vast building via the lift and the long winding hallways.

Mr Smalley opened the door and invited them into his compact but adequate apartment. "Come in. Please, take a seat on the sofa. It's only a two-seater, but I'm sure you ladies won't mind. Can I get you a tea or coffee or a cold drink? I think I have some orange squash in the cupboard somewhere."

"No, don't worry, we had a drink before we left the station."

He sat in the high armchair opposite them, and Sally couldn't help notice how agitated he seemed. His hands were on the go all the time.

"Mr Smalley, there's no need to be nervous, you're not in any trouble. We're here to see what you can tell us about your neighbours, so hopefully it won't prove too taxing for you."

He relaxed into his chair and clenched his shaking hands

together. "Okay, is this to do with the explosion that occurred earlier this year?"

"Possibly, although we've yet to have that confirmed. There's no easy way to say this, but I'd rather not skirt around the truth, if that's okay with you?"

"No, that's exactly what I'd expect. Although, I have to tell you, I'm a little concerned about what you're going to say."

"Don't be. Like I said, all we're here to do is see what you can recall about the neighbours who have lived in the row of cottages over the years."

"Is there a particular reason?" He shuffled forward to the edge of his seat.

"During the demolition stage of the site, the builders uncovered the remains of a body."

"What? You must be joking. Where?"

"That's something we're awaiting the results for. The diggers had gone in, so it's a little difficult to pinpoint the actual burial site."

"In one of the gardens, was it?"

"Maybe. We believe it was buried in concrete, perhaps inside the cottage or possibly under a patio."

"Goodness gracious me. I'd say worse than that but I don't like swearing in front of ladies."

"It's okay, we're not easily shocked as we've heard it all over the years. What can you tell us about your neighbours?"

"Now you're asking. How far back are you expecting me to go? Because the mind isn't what it used to be, I'm in my late seventies now."

"Anything you can tell us will be a huge help. We had a chat with Mrs Lamont who lives in one of the cottages across the road. She was quite helpful, but some of the details she gave us were a little bit sketchy."

He rolled his eyes. "I know the one you mean, she's a nosey parker, that one, always has been. I'd take some of what she told you with a pinch of salt. I think she's fallen out with just about everyone in the community at one time or another, so she's more than likely to have embellished the truth beyond all recognition, that's my take on it."

"Oh, I see. Well, in that case, anything you can tell us about your neighbours will be most welcome."

"Let's see how far back I can go, then."

Over the next ten minutes, his memory did him proud, going back fifty to sixty years to when he was a child. He told them that he'd moved into his cottage with his parents and his brother when he was five. Both his parents had passed away at a relatively young age, forty-eight and forty-five and, being the eldest, he had inherited number two. He'd also raised his sister and brother under that roof until they were old enough to fend for themselves. He'd saved hard over the years and helped to fund their first steps away from the family home. Unfortunately, like his parents, his brother and sister both died young, and he was the only one left.

"I'm so sorry for your loss. You've had a tough life, Mr Smalley," Sally said. She gulped down the lump that had appeared in her throat.

"I have, but I've never let it get the better of me. I try to take one day at a time. I've lived life to the full and have never had any regrets."

"Have you ever been married?"

"Nope, no woman ever stuck around long enough when I was younger, you know, bringing up my brother and sister, them's the breaks, eh? By the time they'd left home, I was too stuck in my ways to consider dating or searching for a wife. I'm not sure I've missed out on much, judging by what I've heard around here. Listening to tales about the downright miserable lives some of these buggers have led with their partners. Sometimes life deals you a hand that you're better off having and one that in the end keeps you sane by all accounts, that's my opinion on the subject, anyway."

"I suppose if you never found the right person to share your life with, you're going to regard things differently to someone who has."

"Probably. I take it you're happily married?"

Sally's cheeks warmed under his gaze. "I am, to a very special man. Actually, we both are. But it took us both a failed marriage to before we finally found our true loves."

"What you're telling me is you had to kiss a lot of frogs before Prince Charming came into your lives and swept you off your feet."

Sally laughed. "Something like that. Getting back to your neighbours before you embarrass me further. What can you tell me about who lived next door to you?"

"At number four? Right, well, early on that was old lady Foster. A spinster through and through with no living relatives. Sadly, her father died in the war, and her mother passed away from a broken heart a few years later. She was all right in tiny doses, a bit miserable now and then. She passed away in her fifties, and the cottage was bought by the Coppells."

Sally noticed Lorne scribbling away in her notebook beside her and waited for her to stop before she asked the next question, "Ah, yes, Mrs Lamont mentioned them. What can you tell us about the Coppell family?"

"Anything and everything. He was a weird one, that one. Most days he ignored you but every now and again he felt the need to stop and have a word with you. He was always nosing over my fence. I didn't have much of a garden, it was mostly filled with raised beds full of veggies. I didn't fancy getting one of those allotments miles from where I live. He used to spend most of his spare time in the man-shed at the bottom of the garden. When he wasn't yelling at Tina and the girls. The night-time was the worst." He shook his head in disgust as the memories must have filled his mind.

"In what respect?"

"All the shouting going on. I think most days she gave as good as she got. I'd hear the kids crying, shouting for their parents to stop, and then the furniture would start flying. Of course, in those days, you coppers never wanted to know about domestic problems, therefore it would have been a waste of time calling nine-nine-nine. I went round there at the very start, the first time I realised what was going on, but really didn't want to get involved after that."

"May I ask why?"

His head dipped, and he clutched his hands together until his knuckles whitened. "Because he threatened me," he mumbled.

"In what way?" Sally asked.

"Told me he'd knock seven bells of crap out of me if I interfered in his marriage again."

"And the abuse went on for how long?"

"I didn't mention abuse, *you* did. One night he just took off. Tina told me he up and vanished. I asked her several times, right up to the day she left, if she'd ever heard from him. She told me no and it was good riddance to bad rubbish. I had to agree with her. From what I could see and hear, he was a pain in the rear most days."

"What happened to Tina and her family?"

He raised his head, and a smile forced his lips apart. "She finally met a decent man on a night out."

"And?"

"And, he refused to move in with her, said the house had a bad vibe about it because of the abuse Coppell had put her through. She had no hesitation in putting a For Sale sign up outside."

"Do you have a forwarding address for her?" Sally asked,

again to ensure every angle was covered and to see if anything matched to the database.

"I don't. I can check but I'm pretty sure I don't have one."

"If you would."

He stood and crossed the room to a cabinet in the corner and pulled a sticky drawer open that squeaked its objection. "Damn thing. I'll get around to fixing that one of these days." Removing an address book, he flipped through a couple of pages then tapped his finger. "No, there's nothing under Coppell, and I don't know the other fella's surname, the man she set up home with."

"That's a shame. Thanks for trying. Did she have a job?"

"No, she was at home all day. Saw to her husband and her kids' needs."

"What about him, do you know where he worked?"

He settled down in his seat and stared at the wall to the side of him. "You're going to have to give me a few minutes to think about that."

Sally could imagine the cogs turning at a slow speed in his mind.

"Wait, I think he worked in some kind of factory. Yes, it's all coming back to me now. I think he was some sort of manager at a place out in Mundford. Do you know it?"

"Is that near Thetford Forest?" Sally asked.

"That's the one. Not sure what type of factory it was. He kept regular hours and was home before six every night. The trouble usually started at around seven, so presumably after he'd scoffed his evening meal and before the kids went to bed. Broke my heart to hear them call out, 'Daddy, stop it. Don't hurt her', all the time."

"I bet it did. Do you think the abuse was only aimed at the wife or do you think it included the kids as well?"

"Hard to say, given what I heard. It's incredibly difficult to shut the screams out, they'll live with me forever." He shook his head over and over and sighed. "Appalling for some men to behave like animals. Why? Women don't deserve to be treated that way, no one does, and to put the kids through that kind of behaviour as well, it's disgusting, that's what it is."

"Do you know if they had any family in the area and, if so, do you know where they lived?"

"No. I don't think so. If they did, I never knew about them. That poor woman had few to no friends, no one came to visit her from what I could tell. All right, I was out all day and someone might have dropped by and seen her while I was at work, but at the weekends it was only the four of them stuck in that house. He never even took the kids out for a ride, to the seaside or anywhere like that. They never went on holiday either, from what I could tell."

"Do you know what happened to him?"

"One day he was there and the next he was gone. I remember seeing Tina in the back garden around the time. I asked in passing where he was, and she told me he'd up and left them. She didn't seem overly upset about it. I asked her if she'd heard from him a few months later, and she shrugged and said no. I got the impression she was enjoying her newfound freedom. She started work in the baker's around the corner, and a few months after that this bloke started calling on her. From what I could see he treated her right, took her and the kids out at the weekend, the sort of thing normal families do." He smiled as he recalled the facts. "The girls had smiles on their faces for the first time in their young lives. It was heart-warming to see."

"How old were the girls when their father left, do you know?"

"God, now you're asking. I'm not the best at guessing ages, never have been. In their teens... hang on, I think the older one had started work in a shoe shop full-time, on one of those government schemes that used to pay a pittance. The younger one was at the secondary school around the corner."

"We can check into that. See, now that's great information you've supplied us with today."

"I suppose so. Once you get thinking about something it comes easier to the mind, doesn't it?"

"It does. What can you tell us about the other neighbours?"

"That's easy enough. Rita and Roland Evans, lovely couple, they lived two doors down from me in number six. I used to go to the pub with Roland."

"That was nice. Did you ever discuss what was going on at number four?"

"Not really. Men don't tend to gossip." He grinned. "We leave that up to you women."

"If you say so. What about his wife, Rita did you say?"

"That's right. She was a super lady, a cook at the local primary school. Very slim, she was, always appeared to be well-dressed in spite of her role. Shall we say she didn't live up to the stereotypical cook or chef, working in an establishment like that."

"Did she ever mention the shouting or screaming that took place next door?"

"No, never. I think they were a couple who preferred to live life without getting involved in confrontations or unnecessary unpleasantness. You could say a bit like me in that respect."

"Okay, and finally, the residents at number eight?"

"That would be Ivy Bailey. Another gem of a lady. Was married young but lost her husband in an accident at work. I've definitely got her address in my little book, wait a moment while I look it up for you." He swished through the pages, found nothing, tutted and eventually located it at the front. "Damn thing, two pages must have been stuck together. Here it is. She was lucky enough to move in with her daughter a few months back. If they hadn't given her the option to live with them, I think she had an eye on moving in here with me. Er, so to speak, not in this actual apartment with me, but the building. Oh dear, I'll shut up, I think I've said enough already. Getting all tongue-tied, I am."

Sally smiled and Lorne noted down the address. "I understood what you meant. Mrs Lamont told me that her daughter had put on an extension for her."

"That's right. Still giving her some independence, but the family would be on call if she needed them, should anything untoward happen to her. She's got a lot of life ahead of her, that one, I can tell you. Very fit lady. Walks miles every week. She and her husband used to be fell walkers back in the day, took off up the Lakes or over to Snowdonia as and when they could. Came back tanned and rejuvenated, whereas me, I would have been laid up for a week, dead on my feet with dozens of blisters to deal with. Not them, their motto was always 'live life to its fullest'."

"And after her husband died?"

"She kept up her walking, just on the flat around Norfolk. She confided in me one day, said it wasn't the same without him. I told her to get back on the horse and to get out there again. Go back to the places she used to visit when he was alive, but she was having none of it. Said they were special times and could never be recreated now that her soulmate was gone. Poor woman. Still, she's with her family now, I'm sure she's better off with them. Loved the company of others, she did."

"We're going to head off to see her soon, she's on our list for visiting today."

"Aww... that's nice. Tell her I said hello, if you wouldn't

mind. She's got my number. If she wants to meet up for a cuppa, tell her to give me a ring."

"I'll be sure to pass on the message. Is there anything else you can tell us?"

Lorne angled her notebook in Sally's direction, and she read the sentence that had been underlined.

"Ah, yes, thanks for the prompt, Sergeant. What about any possible extensions at either number four or six?"

His eyes turned to slits. "I don't recall number four ever having anything, either before or after the Coppells were there, but Rita and Roland definitely had an extension put on the back, took up about a third of the garden, it did. They had one of those brick-built conservatories, well, it was half brick and glass. Although saying that, they incorporated the kitchen into it as well."

"I don't suppose you can remember when it was built, can you?"

"Gosh, let me take a moment to think about it... Okay, I'm inclined to believe it was either in ninety-nine or two thousand. But you'll have to ask them about the specific date."

"That's brilliant, you've been extremely helpful, Mr Smalley."

"Aye, I have to tell you I've even surprised myself with the facts I could remember. I hope it's of some use to you. Shocking to think there was a body lying beneath our feet and no one knew about it. Do you know how long it's been down there? It couldn't be from Roman times, could it? I know there was an area discovered not long ago, over on the east coast, but I think all they found was the odd bone or two."

"No, I don't believe so, this was a full skeleton."

"Oh my, it gets worse. All I can say is I'm grateful I didn't dig anything up when I reconstructed my garden, but then, using the raised beds prevented me from digging, so who's to say what I might have found?" He shuddered. "Bugger, it doesn't bear thinking about, does it?"

"No, it's best not to."

"What can you do about it? Was the body buried in suspicious circumstances...? No, don't answer that, it was bound to be, otherwise it would have had a proper burial, in a graveyard, right?"

"You've answered your own question," Sally replied. "Okay, I think we've got more than enough to be going on with now. Thank you for speaking with us today. Sorry the topic wasn't a pleasant one, but what you've told us will hopefully go a long way towards solving this mystery."

"And what a mystery it is."

He showed them to the door, and Sally and Lorne both shook his hand.

"Be happy, Mr Smalley. We're on this earth for such a short time, most people don't get out there and make the most of it."

He smiled. "I hear what you're saying, dear, but I'm a little long in the tooth to start changing things now."

Sally winked at him. "You're never too old. My mum and dad are about your age, they still go out on their boat regularly, enjoying what life has to offer them."

"Good for them. They have each other for company. Hard to have fun on your own at my time of life."

Sally placed a hand on his arm. "Nonsense, I'm sure there are plenty of clubs you can join. What about here? Don't they lay on entertainment now and again?"

"They do, but I don't like to get involved. I suppose embarrassment plays a large part in that."

"Bite the bullet, get involved. You might even enjoy it."

"Maybe I'll give it a try. Now, go on, get out of here, you've got people to see and a crime to solve."

Sally squeezed his arm and smiled. "Take care of yourself. Here's my card if you ever need to chat."

"Thank you, but don't worry about me, lass." He closed the door behind them.

"What a lovely man," Sally said once they began retracing their steps back to the car.

"I could tell you had a soft spot for him," Lorne teased.

"I did not. Don't tell me the story about his childhood didn't pull at your heartstrings."

"All right, maybe it did. At least he gave us a few things to chase up."

"He did. It's always nice when you question a willing interviewee. While I drive over to Ivy Bailey's, why don't you ring the station, get the team started on searching for the factory where Coppell worked? You can also see if there's any news on the missing person angle for him yet."

"I'm getting a sneaky suspicion that it's him, aren't you?"

"I'm trying to keep an open mind, but it's looking more and more likely to be him. Maybe there's far more to come to light."

"I think you're spot on. Let's hope Ivy can fill in a few missing details for us, or the Evanses come to that."

"I know something."

Lorne faced her and frowned. "What?"

"By the end of tomorrow I'm going to be pissed off asking the same question over and over again."

Lorne laughed. "Yep, and I'm going to get fed up jotting down the same notes. However, we must keep positive. If we don't, we're liable to miss a possible significant clue."

"You're right, as usual."

They exited the building, and Sally paused to look up and catch some of the sun's rays.

"This is nice. I'm in desperate need of a holiday."

"Don't, I honestly can't remember the last time Tony and I went away."

"Maybe you'll be able to get some much-needed time off soon now that you've got a trustworthy manager running the kennels, unless you've changed your mind about her."

"I haven't. Abby has slotted in so well. All the dogs love her, which is unusual."

They reached the car, and Sally frowned. "May I ask why?"

"It's not uncommon for at least one pup to have reservations about a newcomer."

"Ah, I guess that's never really occurred to me before. It would seem I have a lot to learn about a rescue dog's behaviour."

Sally slipped into the car and turned the ignition key. At the same time, Lorne rang the station and put the phone on speaker.

"Hi, Joanna, it's Lorne. How's it going there? Anything to report?"

Joanna's voice filled the car. "Not really. I chased Miss-Pers. They have categorically told us that Paul Coppell wasn't registered as missing with them."

"How strange. Okay, well, we might have learnt the reasoning behind that."

"Oh, care to share?"

"I was getting around to it, sorry, I was a little distracted by the boss's wayward driving for a moment or two."

"Sodding cheek," Sally complained. "Don't listen to her, Joanna. There's nothing wrong with weaving in and out of cars if there's a Sunday driver ticking me off."

Joanna sniggered. "If you say so, boss."

Lorne laughed. "Yeah, that's her side of events. As I was saying before I felt my life was teetering on the edge of danger..."

"Good grief, I've heard it all now," Sally said. She tapped her fingers on the steering wheel. "Are you going to share this revelation with Joanna or not?"

"Given the chance, yes. We had a chat with the bloke who lived at number two. He's revealed that there was some kind of abuse going on in the home; he thinks it was mostly aimed at Mrs Coppell but couldn't tell us if the two children were ever touched, although he did overhear Coppell shouting at them regularly."

"Shit," Joanna said. "In that case, who can blame her for not reporting him missing? What happened?"

"Apparently, we've yet to have it verified by the family, Mr Smalley believes he did a moonlit flit and hasn't been seen since, as far as he knows. This is where it becomes cloudy. He also told us that the wife started work at the local baker's and met a new beau. They moved not long after."

"Hmm... it all sounds like a huge coincidence to me, or am I speaking out of turn?"

"The boss and I came to the same conclusion. I guess we won't know the truth until we track down the former Mrs Coppell or discover the identity of the deceased. Something else we learnt today was that Coppell used to work at some kind of factory over in Mundford. Can you do some digging? See what type of factories are out that way or if any used to be around there and have since closed down."

"Sure, I'll get on it right away. Do you need anything else?" Joanna asked.

"Not right now, Joanna," Sally said. "Let us know what you find out. We're not far from the next location now. We'll see what Ivy Bailey has to say before we make the decision to go to Norwich to call on Rita and Roland Evans. Talking of which, can you check with the council, see if they obtained planning permission for an extension at the rear of number six?" she asked.

"Are you thinking that's where the body was buried?" Joanna said, immediately cottoning on to what Sally was getting at.

"Possibly. We believe it was either buried under number four or number six, until we get a definitive idea from SOCO."

"Again, we'll get on it right away, boss. Anything else? I'll get a printout of Google Street View, see if that helps."

"Good idea. That's it for now, Jo. Thanks. No, wait, you can get Jordan to chase the pathologist, see if there's any news there. I haven't had a chance to check my emails yet, so there's every possibility the PM report has been sent and I haven't picked it up yet, but I doubt it."

"Will do, boss. It can't hurt to chase it."

"Exactly. Speak soon, if not before," Sally agreed. She nodded, gesturing to Lorne to end the call.

WITHIN TEN MINUTES, they pulled up outside a very neat detached home on the edge of Ashill, a small village just north of Watton. The cottage had a thatched roof that appeared to be brand-new, and there was the obligatory abundantly blooming rose, growing up some trellis to the side of the front door.

Sally inhaled a waft of the fragrance as they walked up the long, crazy-paving path. On either side were beds full of summer colour, anything from dahlias to geums and every-thing in between, plus there was a small patch of finely cut lawn on both sides of the path. "I could stay here all day. It's wonderful, isn't it? Must be good for the soul to work and sit in this gem."

"Glorious. Hey, this must be a sign of old age if we're going over the top about a cottage garden."

"You speak for yourself, I've always been one to praise

81

nature when it puts on a good show for us. It has nothing to do with my age, cheeky cow."

Lorne chuckled. "Mention age and stand back. It's like lighting touchpaper every single time."

Sally rang the bell and whispered, "Bollocks," behind her hand just in case someone was watching them from the front window.

A woman in her mid-thirties opened the door. She had a friendly smile and was drying her hands on a tea towel. "Hello. Oh yes, damn, I'd forgotten you were supposed to be coming to see Mum today. You are the police, aren't you?"

Sally and Lorne showed their warrant cards.

"We are. DI Sally Parker, and this is my partner, DS Lorne Warner. No need to apologise, it happens all the time when we ring ahead. Is your mother available to speak with us?"

"Yes, the chiropodist has been to see her this morning. She's in her little annexe. I'll take you through to her. I'm Helen by the way."

"Would you like us to remove our shoes?" Sally asked.

"No, it'll be fine, unless you've been in a muddy field, I'm not that particular about that sort of thing. I have tiled floors throughout the downstairs, mainly because we have dogs, or should I say *had* a dog. Sadly, we lost old Rex a few weeks ago, and I can't bring myself to take on another rescue."

"I'm sorry for your loss. If you do reconsider, my partner here runs a small kennel for abandoned dogs."

"You do? And you're a full-time copper as well? How do you manage to cope with the demands of both jobs?"

"It was a struggle for a while. My husband and I run it together, but now he's working full-time as a property developer, we've had to employ a young lady as a kennel manager. Abby's wonderful. No pressure from me, you're welcome to come and see the dogs anytime you like. You're going to need time to grieve first, though. How old was Rex when he passed?"

"Fourteen, we brought him home as a puppy. He was a Dalmatian."

"That was a good age, he must have been a very contented pooch."

"He was. A treasured member of the family who went everywhere with us. Mum was really upset when he passed. If anything, she's the one who keeps hounding me for another dog, not the kids. She's wearing me down slowly. Have you got a card? When would be the best time to call and see you?"

"In your own time. When you want, Abby will look after you during the day, or if you prefer to come in the evening, either my husband Tony or I can introduce you to the dogs. They're all wonderful, all homeless through no fault of their own. Most of them were bought by people working from home during the lockdown."

"Horrendous and so bloody irresponsible to take on a puppy or older dog, knowing that they would return to work soon. It's the dogs who suffer in the end."

"So true. They're all in good health. We've worked hard to give them their confidence back; being dumped in the kennels can destroy their spirits. Hopefully, there will always be people like you who are willing to give them a new home. Umm… that's not me being pushy."

"I didn't take it that way. I like you, Sergeant. I'll have a word with the family and get back to you soon."

"No rush, we have plenty of dogs for you to choose from, all different personalities. Always better to come and visit a couple of times to make sure the one you choose will be the right one for your family."

"Ah, yes, of course. We'll turn up en masse, if that's okay, then?"

"We'll look forward to seeing you."

"Mum's through here." Helen showed them through the narrow hallway out into the large open-plan kitchen and through the back door. On her immediate right was an L-shaped extension that had a lovely view of the back garden which was equally as pretty as the front.

"I have to say, your gardens are simply beautiful," Sally said, her gaze taking in the glorious beds and the structure within the garden that led the eye to the open fields beyond.

"Why thank you. I've been a keen gardener since I got married. Now Mum is living with us, she helps to keep it in tiptop condition. I do all the labour-intensive chores, like cutting the lawn and the odd hedge here and there, while she potters around, deadheading and watering in the evening. It's a credit to both of us, not just me. I'll be sure to pass on your compliment, too." She knocked on the glass pane in the front door and then entered the small kitchen area to the annexe. "Mum, it's me. I've got two ladies from the police with me. Is it all right to come in?"

"Yes, come through. I'm tidying up the lounge."

Helen rolled her eyes. "She never sits still, and no, her lounge isn't messy."

Sally smiled. "Bless her. How has she settled in since the move?"

"Fine, she loves spending time in here on her own but often wanders over to be with us in the evening. She has her main meal with us. The kids love having her around, only because she spoils them rotten."

"As every grandparent should," Sally said. "I think my parents would be the same if I had any children."

"Why don't you? Is it because of the job?" Helen tilted her head and queried.

"Personal preference, we'll leave it there." Sally smiled awkwardly.

"I'm sorry, I can be a tad nosey at times. My husband makes a habit of slapping me down about it." Helen opened the door to a cosy lounge, a room about ten feet square. Ivy didn't have much furniture in the room, so it didn't look cramped at all. "Mum, this is DI Sally Porter and DS Lorna Watkins."

Sally laughed. "Near enough, it's Sally Parker and Lorne Warner."

"Damn, I'm useless with names, forget my kids' and my husband's most of the time. Mum will vouch for me, won't you?"

"Oh yes, glad she only has to remember to call me Mum, even then sometimes she has to pause to think about it. Come in, take a seat. Are you going to stop, love?" Ivy asked her daughter.

"I wasn't, but I will if you would prefer me to."

Ivy glanced at Sally and Lorne and shook her head. "No, you get off, I'm sure I'll be fine with these lovely ladies."

"I'm sure you will. Give me a shout if I can be of assistance. Sorry, I should have asked, can I get you a drink? Tea or coffee?"

Sally smiled. "Kind of you to offer, but we're fine."

Helen left the annexe, and Sally and Lorne sat in the two-seater sofa opposite Ivy's comfy armchair.

"Right, now how can I help you today? I must say, I was surprised to get the call from you."

"It's nothing to be alarmed about, we're simply following up on some enquiries about your old property."

"Oh, what can you mean? I thought that place would have been bulldozed by now. Has something happened, like squatters moved in?"

"Nothing like that. You're right, the construction work has started on the site, yesterday morning in fact. Unfortunately, work ground to a halt soon after."

"Oh, well, don't stop there. You must tell me why."

Sally inhaled a large breath and let it seep out between her teeth. "Because a skeleton was found at the scene."

"What? How? Who did it belong to? If you get what I mean? I'm not sure I understand, not really. Please forgive me, the mind isn't what it used to be. Please, I don't feel well, can you get my daughter?"

Lorne bolted for the door before Sally had the chance to issue the order. She returned with Helen a few moments later. Sally had moved to sit on the arm of Ivy's chair and had an arm around her shoulder when they both burst into the room. She leapt out of her seat and let Helen take her place.

"Mum, whatever is wrong?"

"Get me one of my heart tablets, love, you know, one of the blue ones in the small tub beside my bed."

"I'll be right back." Helen shot out of the room and came back with one of the pills along with a glass of water and handed them to her mother to take. "Here you go." After seeing to her mother's needs, she faced Sally and asked, "What on earth did you say to her?"

Breathing heavily, her mother said, "You mustn't blame them, not really. It was the shock, that's all."

"I don't understand, what shock?" Helen demanded. She took the glass of water from her mother and placed it on the table then gripped her hand. "Will someone please have the decency to tell me what's going on here? I can't bear this bloody silence, knowing that whatever you just told my mother has caused her to feel ill. I have a right to know."

Sally sighed. "You do, if Ivy is okay with me telling you?"

"Yes, yes, get on with it." Ivy clutched her daughter's hand tightly.

Sally went over the story from the beginning, as much as they knew to date. Helen's mouth hung open for a while, apparently lost for words.

Eventually, she shook her head a few times and said, "I don't understand what this has to do with my mother. Care to enlighten us, Inspector?"

"Nothing per se. All we're trying to ascertain are facts about the families who lived in the row of cottages from a few years back. We've just come from visiting Ken Smalley at the sheltered housing where he's now staying—he sends his regards, by the way. He gave us a lot of details about the family who lived next door to him."

"I know who you're talking about, the Coppells, am I right?" Ivy said, her lip curling slightly.

"Absolutely. He told us that Mr Coppell left the house one day, possibly overnight, and never returned. Can you tell us what you know about the incident? If you're feeling up to it, of course."

"I am. He was a vile, narcissistic bastard, and no, I won't apologise for my language, not when I speak about that man. If you can bloody call him that."

"Mum, calm down. I've never seen you so irate before when talking about someone."

"You've never come across an individual as sadistic as he was, love. I kept you away from him, was super-protective over you when he was around."

"When I was at school? Gosh, I remember it well."

"Yes, that's right. The day after he left, I relaxed, all of us did, and we became a proper family again."

"I had totally forgotten about what went on back then, until now. Paige was two years older and Erica two years younger than me. I think Paige had just started working at that shoe shop on a government scheme called Work Experience or something along those lines."

"That's right, she did," Ivy confirmed. "I'm so glad he went off when he did, otherwise Tina might never have run into

Chris and her life would have remained miserable until her dying breath."

"Ken mentioned that Tina started seeing someone. Alas, he couldn't remember his name. Chris what, do you know?"

"Get my handbag, Helen, please. It'll be in the contacts in my phone. They moved in together a few months after they began seeing each other. What was he now?"

Helen passed her mother her handbag, and Ivy clutched at her chest as she reached out for it.

"Damn heart, don't bloody pack in on me, not now."

"Mum, do you have to say things like that? I am here, you know."

"Hush, Helen, I was joking. The pain is easing, there's no need for you to start fussing over me." She opened the zip on her bag and dipped her hand in to find her phone which she removed and then placed her handbag on the floor beside her, in between Helen and herself. "Now let me see if I can find it." She scrolled through her contacts and clicked her thumb and forefinger together. "I've got it. He's in the army. They only got married a couple of years ago, I think they had to wait seven years after that dreadful husband of hers went missing before they could tie the knot. Is that right, Inspector? In the end they left it another few years before signing on the dotted line at the registry office, just to be on the safe side."

Sally waved her hand from side to side. "Kind of. After the seven years have passed, the spouse has to apply for a divorce through the courts, but not until they've made a reasonable attempt to find their missing partner."

Ivy pointed her gnarled finger at Sally. "That's correct. She went through hell, they both did. We stayed in touch after she left number four, and she confided in me that she no longer had the strength to carry on. All she'd ever wanted was to be content and happy within a safe environment and marriage. It was obvious that Coppell could never give her what she wanted, but she was afraid that Chris would get fed up with waiting around and leave her. Silly girl, there's no way Chris would have done that, he loved her. They were meant to be together. I'm so glad they eventually walked down the aisle, they made the perfect couple on the day."

"She's Mrs what these days? We've tried searching our database for Coppell, but nothing has surfaced."

"Lawler, Tina Lawler. I think the younger girl took on Chris's surname, but Paige, the older girl, was already engaged to her lovely young man and decided to stick with Coppell for a few months before it was legally changed when she got married. Needed her head read, getting married at her age. She'd just turned eighteen when she said 'I do'. I believe her husband was the total opposite to her father. I was wrong about them, thought their marriage would never last, but they're still very much in love today, according to Tina."

"When did you last either see or contact Tina?"

"A couple of months ago, it was not long after I moved in here with Helen. We met up for a coffee over which we had a good old gossip. I can honestly say the difference in her was remarkable."

Sally picked up on the sudden change in Ivy. "Are you all right, Ivy? Is there something you're not telling us?"

Ivy plucked a tissue from the box beside her and dabbed at her streaming eyes.

"What is it, Mum? Come on, it's better out than kept inside, doing all sorts of damage."

"Once she proudly announced that Erica was getting married to her long-term boyfriend, they have two kids together, she took hold of my hand and began crying. I was so concerned, I shifted my chair closer to hers, and she whispered that she had cancer and was about to start chemo."

"Oh, Mum, you never said. How awful for her, after all the trauma she's been through in her life. Some people aren't meant to know what true happiness is, are they?"

"That's a damn shame. How did her husband take the news?" Sally asked.

"As expected. He promised to stand by her, that he would do anything and everything to ease the traumatic journey ahead of her. I've stayed in touch with her every couple of weeks over the phone but I haven't actually seen her in the flesh. Her choice, not mine. She told me the chemo hadn't been kind to her appearance and she'd rather not go out in public until she got to grips with her condition herself. It doesn't sound too good, does it?" Ivy reached out and clutched her daughter's hand. "If ever cancer comes calling, let me go, I don't want them pumping all that shit into my body, only for it to fail. There's more to life than ending it with pure torture."

"But if there's a hope of extending your life, why wouldn't you, Mum?" Helen queried.

"Because everyone is different, love. It's not for me, and no one could sit me down and try to persuade me otherwise. I remember what happened to a dear friend of mine, the lady who took me under her wing from my first day at work when I was only seventeen. She rang me one day to say goodbye. Carol had been like a second mum to me, we'd stayed in touch all those years. I was in my thirties when I received the call. I broke down when she whispered goodbye to me. I asked her why. She revealed that she'd had cancer before and had gone through chemo and simply couldn't stand the thought of going through a second bout of it. So she was signing out. I sobbed for days, knowing that I could lose her any day, and I did, less than a week later. Her daughter rang me at Carol's request. Apparently, she died peacefully, with all her family around her."

"That's so sad," Sally said. She wiped away a stray tear. "It's not for everyone. I suppose if your friend had been through the treatment before only for the disease to return, a person is bound to wonder if it's worth all the suffering, just to cling to life for an extra few more years."

"Exactly. She couldn't put her family through it again either. I still miss her today. I fear we've veered off the path somewhat."

Sally smiled and patted her hand. "It sometimes does us good to veer off the track now and again. How are you feeling now?"

"Like death warmed up, but I'll plod on, I always do. You'll be wanting Tina's address, I shouldn't wonder."

"That would be great, if you don't mind, and thank you for warning us that she is ill. It makes a difference to meet someone and be forewarned."

"That's what I thought. Will you tell her I'm thinking of her? I think she realises that anyway, but it wouldn't hurt to let her know again. I send her a bunch of flowers every Friday just to put a smile on her face for the weekend."

"Again, I didn't know that, Mum. What's with all the secrecy?"

"It's not a secret, not really, love. Simply me showing a good friend that I care, there's no harm in that. What am I going to do with all that money sitting in my bank account, take it with me?"

"I suppose you're right. I've told you over and again that I don't want it."

"You refused to take it when this place was built. I know you'll get it all eventually. In the meantime, I wanted to do some good with it rather than the money sitting in the bank accruing a miserable interest rate, although that's much better than it was a few years ago."

"All right, Mum, it's your money, you can do with it what you like. I'm not having a go at you."

"Good."

The mother and daughter smiled at one another, and Ivy ran a hand over Helen's cheek.

"You've been the best daughter ever. This place proves how much I mean to you, but when the time comes, I want you to let me go, dear. No pangs of guilt or anything daft like that."

"Do we have to hold this conversation right now, Mum? I'm sure the officers don't want to hear us being all soppy with each other and ending up in tears."

"Yes, you're right." Ivy held her phone out so Lorne could jot down the details they needed for their next stop.

Sally leaned over to have a peek. "Dereham, that's not too far, we could nip over there now."

Lorne nodded.

"Unless there's anything else you can tell us, Ivy? I don't want to push you too much, not if you're not feeling well."

"I'm fine, getting better by the second. What about this body? Can you tell us more about that?"

Sally paused and then decided not to say anything further about the skeleton, aware of how unfavourable the news might be to Ivy's health. "There's really not a lot we can add at this stage. The pathologist and her team are doing their best to find out who the remains belong to."

Helen gasped and slapped a hand over her gaping mouth. She stared at Sally. Ivy glanced at her daughter, and Sally took the opportunity to warn Helen not to pursue things further with a firm shake of the head.

"Whatever is the matter, Helen?" Ivy asked.

"Sorry, I don't know what came over me, silly me. As you were. Will that be all now, Inspector? I think Mum's had enough excitement for one day."

Sally and Lorne stood, and Sally smiled down at the mother and daughter.

"It is. We can't thank you enough for supplying us with Tina's address. Take care of yourselves."

"I'll show you out," Helen said. "We have to go back through the house, the back gate is permanently locked as extra security for Mum."

Ivy reached out a hand to shake Sally's. "Good luck. I'm sorry I wasn't more help to you."

Sally patted the back of Ivy's hand. "I'm sorry to have caused you all this extra stress. Take good care of yourself."

"You didn't, not really. Goodbye."

Once they had left the annexe and entered the main house again, Helen turned to ask, "The body, you don't think it's him, do you?"

Sally shrugged. "Until we get a formal identification, we won't be able to say one way or another."

"I remember him being a wicked man. His eyes bored into yours if he saw you pass the cottage. He used to stand at the lounge window all the time, scowling at everyone who walked past. Horrible, vile man. What if it does turn out to be him?"

"Then that's when our investigation will truly begin."

Helen chewed on her lip and shook her head. "Tina wouldn't have done it, she wouldn't have had either the strength or the courage to have taken his life. You'll see what I mean when you meet her."

"And the daughters were how old when he went missing?"

"God, now you're asking. Let me see if I can work that out." Her brow wrinkled, and she held up her fingers and tapped them as she counted. "This is only a rough guess. Paige would have been sixteen or seventeen and Erica about twelve or thirteen. You'll really need to ask them or their mother when you interview them. It's so sad that she's in ill health at the moment, she deserves so much better. That new fella of hers is a real gem, so she can take heart from that."

"We'll pop over there and see her now. Thanks again to you and your mother for seeing us. Sorry our meeting caused your mother to have one of her attacks. It's never our intention to put people under that much stress."

"Don't worry, the tablets keep her stable. She'll be fine in an hour or so. We're glad we could be of some assistance. Giving you Tina's address will hopefully help your investigation go in the right direction. Please, be gentle with her when you do meet with her. Everyone in the area knew what that horrible man was up to when he lived there. The three of them must have been terrified most days."

"Don't worry, we'll be gentle. Even if they went to hell and back that's no reason to bump Coppell off, or do you think otherwise?"

"No, that isn't what I'm saying at all. Just ignore me, I was too young to really understand what was going on back then."

Sally smiled. "I'm not usually the type to jump in feet first, my team and I will do the necessary background digging as usual before we decide who the guilty party is. Because, if it does turn out to be him, it's obvious that someone killed him. A body doesn't appear in concrete overnight all by itself."

"I hear you. All I'm saying is… those girls were living through hell on earth, and that should be considered before you take any action against anyone, shouldn't it? They were prisoners in their own home, it was only a matter of time before he killed someone. Maybe one of them got in first, predicting what would happen and dealing with the situation before it was too late. Like I said, ignore me, I'm probably talking a lot of bloody nonsense. A word of warning, if I may, unless you've lived through domestic violence yourself, I don't think any of us has the right to judge how someone deals with the aggressor."

Sally stared at Helen, the cruel images of when she used to be married to her heartless first husband, Darryl, rattling through her mind. He'd been an evil, callous bastard, who'd beaten her daily, raped her, and even after she'd plucked up the courage to speak out about him and got him arrested and put in prison, he'd come after her. Okay, all that was firmly in the past, but hearing what Coppell was capable of was bringing it all back to her by the bucketload.

"Thanks again for your help," Lorne's voice broke through her reverie.

Shaking her head to rid herself of the images, Sally shook Helen's hand. "Here's my card if you should need to speak to me further. Take care, Helen."

"Hopefully that won't be necessary. I'll keep it safe in case we need it. Good luck with the investigation, we're happy to have played a part, however small."

"I can't tell you how much this visit has meant to us. Goodbye, Helen."

"Goodbye, fingers crossed you get to the bottom of what actually happened." Helen closed the door.

Sally and Lorne walked back to the car, and it wasn't until they were seated inside that Lorne faced her and said, "That brought back a slew of memories you'd successfully buried all these years, I can tell. Are you all right?"

"I'm fine, determined to find out the truth. As tempted as I was to knife Darryl at times, I didn't go through with it. The thought of robbing Darryl of his life prevented me from doing it a number of times. No one but God has the authority to do that."

"If that's what you believe... On the other hand, everyone has their limits, we need to take that into consideration as well. Furthermore, this case is different to yours."

95

"In what way?" Sally turned to ask.

Lorne shrugged. "Take a second to think about it."

She paused, and Sally did that, but didn't offer any response.

"There were kids involved," Lorne said. "The need to protect them would have come into the equation, wouldn't it?"

"Ah, yes, I'm with you now. Perhaps we won't know the answer to that until we've interviewed Tina. Do you think we should call ahead or show up unannounced? That's the one dilemma running through my mind at the moment."

"I prefer the element of surprise in cases like this."

"So do I. Let's go then. Can you do the honours and enter the details into the satnav? I'll head off in that direction. Or perhaps we should consider having a spot of lunch first?" Sally said after noticing it was almost one-thirty.

"I'm okay if you are. We're bound to get offered a drink when we get there, that will be sufficient for me. My stomach is tied up in knots as it is. Shoving food down my neck might turn out to have devastating consequences."

Sally laughed. "You are funny. I was only talking about having a sandwich, not a full blowout."

"Either way, I don't think I could stomach anything, but you go ahead if you want something."

"I'll pass and hope there's a drink on offer at the other end. Sod's law is telling me there won't be."

They both laughed.

"Maybe we should pick up a bottle of water or juice on the way, just in case."

CHAPTER 4

$\mathcal{L}$orne rang the bell to the detached house positioned
in a quiet close on a small estate on the outskirts of
Dereham. Sally removed her warrant card from her
pocket in readiness. It took a while for the door to open.

A woman peered around the gap. She had a scarf on, and
Sally concluded it was to cover her loss of hair during her
treatment. Ivy had told her that Tina was afraid to be seen in
public these days.

"Yes. What do you want?"

"Hello, Tina. It is Tina, isn't it?"

"Yes, that's right. Tina Lawler, and you are?"

"I'm DI Sally Parker, and this is my partner, DS Lorne
Warner. We're from the Norfolk Constabulary. Would it be
possible to come in and have a quick chat with you?"

A frown wrinkled her brow above where her eyebrows
used to sit. "About what?"

"It's a personal matter. I promise we won't take up much
of your time."

"How did you get this address?"

Sally thought that was a strange question for her to ask.

"We were at Ivy Bailey's house not long ago, and she gave us your new surname and address."

"I'm confused. My new surname? I'm remarried, I didn't change it intentionally, if that's what you're getting at?"

"I'm not. Please, can we come in and have a chat with you?"

"Very well, if you must. I'm not dressed for visitors. I'm going through treatment, so I'm not going to make excuses for how I look."

"So we've heard. Can you manage okay?"

The woman was stooped over a walking stick and hobbled up the hallway. "Yes, don't worry about me. I'm used to dealing with the pain and the unwillingness of my legs to work properly. I need to get to my chair, quickly."

"You go, we'll shut the door and follow you in." Sally did the decent thing and removed her shoes.

Lorne did the same, and then they joined Tina in the large lounge. On one side of the room was a bay window overlooking the village green. Tina had made herself comfortable in a squishy easy chair close to a three-seater sofa.

"Take a seat. If you want a drink, you'll have to make it yourselves as I'm not up to doing it."

"We're fine for now. How are you doing?" Sally asked. "Ivy mentioned that you're going through chemo, oh, and she sends you her regards."

"I'm as expected, in the circumstances. I don't understand. Why were you at Ivy's earlier, and why did she give you my address?"

Sally smiled and sank onto the sofa. Lorne extracted her notebook, ready to jot down any information that Tina was willing to share with them.

"Well, yesterday we were called out to investigate a scene at a building site."

Tina's brow knitted again. "And what has this got to do with me?"

"The location was the row of cottages at Watton, where you used to live."

"Oh, okay. I still don't know what it has to do with me. I left there around eighteen years ago, or thereabouts."

"We're visiting all the previous owners of the homes in that vicinity."

"Okay, but why?"

Sally inhaled a breath and let it out slowly. "Because a body was discovered at the site. Actually, it was a skeleton that was exposed."

Tina's head jutted forward. "What did you say?"

"A skeleton was found when the builders began excavating the site. They had to stop working, it's the law when remains are uncovered at a location. The pathologist and Forensics were brought in to investigate the scene."

"Bloody hell. I still don't understand what this has to do with me."

Sally noticed how much Tina's hand was shaking in her lap. "Well, as I said, it's our job to question the former residents of the site to find out what they might know about the body."

"Why would I know anything? Who is it?"

"That much we don't know. We're waiting for the post-mortem report to come through before we can ascertain that. However, the pathologist has given us a preliminary indication that the remains belong to a male."

"Goodness me. I wonder who that could be. A skeleton, you say. Does that mean the body has been buried there for years? Perhaps before the properties were even built?"

"That's correct. Again, that's what we're trying to figure out. Do you have any idea who the remains may belong to?"

She held Sally's gaze for a second or two. "No idea at all.

Can you tell me where it was found? There were four cottages there. Wait, this couldn't have anything to do with the gas explosion, could it?"

"We don't believe so. There's speculation that the body was buried in concrete some years ago. We've narrowed it down to being buried at number four or number six."

"I lived at number four. How strange."

Tina sounded convincing enough. She was answering all of Sally's questions, not dodging any, as someone guilty of murder might do.

"How long did you live there?"

"We moved there when we first got married. I was twenty at the time, I'm sixty-two now."

"So that would have been in the early eighties then?"

"Yes, I think either eighty-one or eighty-two. Before that a middle-aged couple lived there with two kids. They bought a bigger house around the Norwich area, I believe."

"Do you remember their names?"

"I don't. The damn chemo has fried my brain cells in places, I can tell you."

"I'm sure. Don't worry, we can look up the deeds to the property, if necessary. Speaking with your former neighbours over the last couple of days, they gave us the impression that your former husband left the marital home one day and didn't return, is that correct?"

Her chin dipped to her chest, and her hands twisted around each other in her lap. The first sign of possible nerves that Sally had detected.

"Yes, that's right. I don't really like talking about him."

"May I ask why?" Of course Sally was aware of the reason, but getting the information from the horse's mouth was always a major advantage to any investigation.

"He wasn't a very nice man. Put me and my two girls through hell."

"Why did he leave?"

Her gaze met Sally's, and she shrugged. "I've been asking myself the same question for years. It didn't make sense at the time and still doesn't, when it crosses my mind, which I have to be honest, isn't that often. But now and then, mainly after I've suffered from the odd nightmare, I lie awake and wonder what happened to the bastard. Maybe he hooked up with a woman and went off with her. I really can't tell you more than that."

"Did he abuse you, Tina?"

Again, her gaze dropped. "Yes, every damn day up until he left."

As a fellow abusee, Sally's heartstrings tugged. "I'm sorry to hear that. How long after your wedding day did the abuse start?"

"I've tried to pinpoint the trigger over the years, but nothing has really come to mind. I suppose if you pushed me, I would have to say it surfaced after Erica was born, she's my youngest. I felt for my daughters. He could do what he liked to me, and I assure you he did, however, I did everything I could to prevent him laying his hands on my daughters. They wouldn't have deserved that."

"And did you succeed? Did he ever lay a hand on your girls?" Sally probed.

"No, maybe he lashed out at them here and there but he didn't... rape them, I'm pretty sure of that. Not that I've plucked up the courage to ask them over the years. I felt it best to leave the subject well alone. Why bring back all those bad memories when the girls have always been happy...? Well, since the day he left. Knowing that has meant the world to me. Although saying that, I think me marrying Chris has been the making of them. Given the girls a fantastic role model. Both girls married when they were quite young. Paige had just turned eighteen, she'd been seeing Ian for years."

"Do your daughters have any children?" Sally asked, relieved to hear that neither of her daughters had mental health issues which was pretty common when dealing with domestic abuse cases.

"Unfortunately, Paige has never wanted any kids. Erica has two. A boy, Leo, is six, and a girl, Corally, is four. They've been together around ten years but only just tied the knot. Which was fine by me. Youngsters these days often do things the wrong way round, don't they?"

Sally laughed. "They do indeed. Tell me, have you ever heard from your ex?"

"No. In some ways I wish I had in the beginning, it would have made marrying Chris a whole lot easier. As it was, with him vanishing the way he did, I had to wait seven years plus another year on top before I could divorce him."

"Very strange. Do you think that was his intention, to go off and leave you in limbo as it were?"

"Probably. Narcissistic bastard until the bitter end. Why change a habit of a lifetime?"

"Did he show any signs of violent behaviour while you were dating?"

"No, nothing at all. He couldn't have been nicer to me. Yes, he swore and cursed when someone cut him up in the car, doesn't everyone? The alarm bells didn't start ringing until after the kids were born. They were very demanding babies, especially during the night. I think he went to work exhausted most days."

"Where did he work?"

"Simmons' Steels over in Mundford, he was a manager there."

"Did he still work there after he walked out on you?"

"No, that was the first place I rang, after I calmed down. They told me they hadn't seen hide nor hair of him since the day he left our house. It didn't surprise me in the slightest and I didn't give it a second thought. Selfish to the core, he was."

"How did the firm react?"

"They were livid, but I get the feeling they were also relieved as well, even though they didn't tell me that."

"Relieved? You have no idea why?"

"No, not in the slightest. As far as I was concerned, he loved his job, so I didn't see any reason for him to walk out on it. It also gave me the foundation to believe he'd taken off with someone and possibly left the area. It wasn't until Chris and I wanted to get married that we started looking for the bastard."

"Did you ever report him missing?"

Tina glanced up and stared at the wall behind Sally. "No, as I said, I thought he'd taken off to live life anew miles away with someone else. There was also the fact that the girls and I weren't living on eggshells all the time. We didn't want him back, that was the deciding factor for me. Should I have reported him missing? Is that what families do when people walk away from their lives?"

"Nine times out of ten, yes."

"Mum, are you in?" a voice called out from the hallway.

"I'm in the lounge, love. Come through. It sounds like Erica. She generally stops in for a cuppa on her way to pick the kids up from school."

A woman with her brunette hair tied back in a ponytail entered the room. "Oh, damn, sorry, you should have told me you were having visitors."

"I didn't know, love. These two ladies are police officers, come to have a chat with me about the old house. It was torn down yesterday."

"I see. Everything all right?" Erica seemed perplexed. "Wait, I'll be right back. Can I get you ladies a drink?"

"I'll have a glass of water," Tina said. "I'm due to take a couple of tablets soon. Ladies, care for a tea or a coffee?"

"A coffee for both of us would be great, white with one sugar. Thank you," Sally replied.

Erica shot out of the room, and Tina smiled.

"Always tearing around in a rush, that girl. She'll have your drinks with you in a flash."

"No problem." Sally revisited the conversation they were having before Erica had showed up. "Going back to why you didn't report him missing."

"I just never considered him missing. So why the dickens would I file a report and waste the police's time searching for him? Can't you get arrested for that?"

"On the odd occasion, it has been known. Did he pack a suitcase? Take any of his belongings with him?"

"At the time I had a brief look around, and no, he left everything there and went. I took that to mean he wanted a fresh start somewhere else. You know, left in a hurry, couldn't get away from us quickly enough."

"I see, and you didn't think that was strange?"

"No, like I said, I thought he couldn't wait to run off with another woman so didn't give two hoots why he wouldn't take his stuff with him. I ended up getting one of those incinerator bins for the garden and burnt all his possessions."

"How soon after he left did you resort to doing that?"

"A couple of weeks. I couldn't bear being surrounded by his stuff, it was a natural progression. It's not like he stayed in touch, rang me to tell me he fancied a breather from the marriage and that he was going to return in a couple of weeks."

Sally nodded. "I agree. In the circumstances, I think you made the right decision. Is there anything of his left?"

"No, I got rid of everything. I wanted rid. What's that song? Oh yes, something about washing a man right out of your hair. The girls helped me, Chris wasn't on the scene then, but the girls did their bit. Actually, we did it in the dark and downed a bottle of fizz between us. It was such a cathartic exercise, for all of us."

The door opened again, and Sally left her seat to relieve Erica of the mugs. "Are these ours?"

"Yes, I fancied a glass of squash, and Mum's is the water." Erica lowered the tray to allow her mother to remove the glass of water, then she placed the tray on the floor and sat on the arm of her mother's easy chair.

Erica cleared her throat and asked, "What's this all about?"

"You're never going to guess, not in a zillion years," Tina said.

"Go on, tell me."

Tina leaned in and touched her forehead against her daughter's. "Well, when the builders excavated the site, they only dug up a bloody skeleton. Can you believe that?" She shuddered. "Saying it out loud has made me go cold all over, that has."

"Bloody hell, seriously? Who is it, do you know?" Erica asked, half an eye on her mother as if gauging her reaction.

"We're waiting on the post-mortem report."

"I don't understand why you're here, care to tell me?"

"It would appear the body was either buried under number four or number six. We're making enquiries to see if any of the previous residents can shed any light into who the person is."

Erica hooked an arm around her mother. "Oh, I see. Any ideas, Mum?"

"No, dear. Before you arrived, the inspector was asking me what happened to your father."

Erica's head swivelled so fast to face Sally that a bone cracked. "What? Why? You don't think... do you?"

Sally shrugged. "Possibly, that's why we're making enquiries. Have you seen or heard from your father since he left?"

Tina held up a finger in front of Erica, preventing her from answering. "I told you, none of us have heard a dickie bird from him. I'm really not liking where this conversation is leading right now. What are you suggesting? Come on, out with it!"

"All we're doing is searching for possible clues that might lead us to identifying the corpse. I'm not denying that I find it intriguing that your husband went missing and has never been heard of since. And yes, we've carried out the necessary checks through our system and drawn a blank."

Erica shook her head slowly. "It can't be him, it just can't be," she shrieked.

The front door slammed, and Tina and Erica shot a glance at each other.

A blonde woman marched into the room. "What in God's name is going on here?"

"Paige. I didn't know you were coming here today. Whatever is the matter, dear? Shouldn't you be at work?"

"I was at work, I left early to be with you, Mum."

Tina frowned. "What? Be here? Why?" She turned to face Erica and demanded, "Did you ring your sister?"

"She did, don't take it out on her. I had a right to know if the police were here hounding you."

Sally raised her hand to speak. "With respect, we're doing no such thing. All we're doing is making general enquiries about when your family lived at the address over in Watton."

"Oh, I see. You're not here to arrest Mum then?" Paige shot a glance at Erica, and her eyes narrowed.

"Sorry, sis. I just thought..." Erica mumbled, and she pulled her mother closer to her.

"You thought?" Sally prompted, trying to read the look shooting between the sisters.

"That you always make an arrest if a body is found and you'd come here to do just that."

"You're wrong. I reiterate, the only reason we're here is to make enquiries. To follow up on the details we've been given thus far during the investigation. It would be remiss of us not to, I'm sure you'll agree."

Paige's shoulders slumped, and her feistiness shrank before Sally's eyes. "I'm sorry, believe me, I'm always jumping the gun. I was only looking out for my mother, she's seriously ill and can do without... well, being questioned by the police."

"I totally get where you're coming from, but you also need to understand our necessity to follow up on certain details that we've already been given."

"I do, I think." Paige collected a dining chair from the other side of the room and placed it beside her mother. She then reached out for one of her hands. Erica linked hands with her mother's other hand.

Sally got the impression that together, the three women could be a force to be reckoned with. "You're obviously very close, even now you're both married."

"Seems an odd statement to make," Paige piped up. "She's our mother, and may I remind you for the second time, that Mum has been to hell and back over the last few months, thanks to bloody cancer. Maybe you'll take that fact into consideration here."

"Now, Paige, don't start," Tina said. "The officers haven't done anything wrong. I haven't felt obligated to answer their questions, not in the slightest."

"Nevertheless, you look exhausted, Mum. I refuse to let them probe any further, not today. You need time to recover in between your chemo sessions. Being hounded by questions is only going to hamper your recovery, surely you can see that, can't you?"

There it was again, that word hounding! *I'm doing nothing of the sort, Tina has answered all my questions willingly. Yes, she might be a touch upset now, but that could be because of the attention her daughters are giving her.*

Sensing Paige's reluctance to allow her mother to continue and possibly end up feeling stressed, Sally decided to put a halt to the visit. "I'm going to leave things there and maybe come and see you again, if I need to, as the investigation develops."

The relief on all the women's faces was evident, but Sally wasn't prepared to think anything of it at this stage. Putting herself in their shoes, coppers showing up unannounced after all these years, questioning her about what Darryl was likely up to, would have unnerved her as well. "One last thing before we go."

"Of course, what's that?" Paige asked, obviously the strongest of the three women when they were all together in the same room.

"Your mother told me that she no longer had any possessions belonging to your father, the three of you burnt them all a few weeks after he left."

"That's right, I remember the night well," Paige confirmed. "What about it?"

"If you had anything remaining tucked away somewhere, we could take it to the lab and try to obtain DNA from it, which will go towards confirming the identification of the deceased."

"There you go again. No means no, Inspector, we don't have anything of his any more. Sorry, but unless you've been the victim of abuse, you will never be able to understand our need to forget about that man. None of us have ever grieved for him since the day he walked out on us. Why would we?

The narcissistic bastard made our lives a living hell every second he was with us."

"I do understand, believe me."

Paige sat erect and forced her shoulders back, her head held high. "How could you? The police never understand a victim's side of the story, they never have and they never will."

"Because… my husband was an abuser as well. So, you see, I totally understand the mixed emotions you have running through you right now, I can assure you."

Paige's shoulders dipped once more. "Then I apologise. You must forgive me. May I ask how you got out of the situation? Your marriage?"

"Eventually, he was dealt with appropriately. It took me a while to find the courage, but one day, when I could no longer stand him raping me, I revealed the truth to my colleagues and he was arrested and went to prison."

"Thank God for that," Tina said nervously. She let out the breath she'd been holding in during Sally's revelation. "Men like that shouldn't be allowed to walk God's earth. Despicable human beings. I never try to think of the girls' father as a *man*, because a true man wouldn't sink to such a low level. He rarely, if ever, spoke out or shouted at a man, it was only ever towards women."

"My ex was the same. They're cowards at the end of the day, amongst other things. However, they need to be dealt with in the correct manner, within the law." Sally left it there and rose from her chair.

The three family members all nodded, and Paige accompanied Sally and Lorne to the front door. They slipped on their shoes and stepped over the threshold to leave.

Sally pulled a card from her pocket and gave it to Paige. "My number, should one of you need it, if only for a simple chat."

"Like for victim's support? Aren't there proper places where we can go for that?" Paige responded brusquely.

"There are. Have you sought out counselling over the years?"

"No, never. We dealt with any pain and anguish that arose in our house, ourselves. We've always been a huge support to each other, no matter what life threw at us."

Sally nodded. "That's great to know. We'll be in touch with your mother soon, if we identify the remains."

"Can I ask you to deal with me rather than worry my mother? You can see how distressing your visit has been for her today. All I'm doing is trying to protect her, especially at this traumatic time, during her sessions of chemo."

"I should have thought about that. Do you want to give me your phone number?"

She reeled it off, and Sally jotted it down in her notebook, then she said goodbye and walked back to the car with Lorne. "Don't say anything until we're in the car," she warned out of the corner of her mouth.

"I wasn't going to. Nice day, shame we've been stuck inside for most of it. Fancy stopping off for that sandwich on the way back?"

"To be honest with you, I don't think I could stomach one. I'll stop at the baker's en route, if you like?"

"If you would. I'll ring the station, see if they've had time to grab anything yet." Lorne rang the team as soon as they returned to the car, leaving Sally staring back at the house, contemplating what the three women had confided in them.

"They haven't had time to eat yet and would welcome us making a detour, if you're intending to go back to the station."

"That's the plan. We need to sit down and go through what we've learnt today. Lots to sift through."

. . .

WHEN THEY RETURNED, Lorne distributed the sandwiches to her colleagues. Joanna was the one who got off her backside to make the coffee for all of them. Back at Tina's home, Sally's had remained untouched, so a fresh brew was most welcome.

Lorne broke off a sliver of her ham and cheese sandwich and slid it across the desk to Sally on a napkin. "Only a small piece, you can't run on fresh air all day."

Smiling, Sally scoffed the granary snack and thought as she chewed.

"What are you thinking, or is that too obvious?" Lorne asked.

"There's more to this than meets the eye, but without a definitive answer about the identification, we're up shit creek. Sod it, we should have dropped over to the lab while we were out."

Her partner squirmed. "My fault, I was thinking about my stomach as usual."

"Nonsense, don't ever think that, we're entitled to eat, even if it's on the go. Jordan, did you manage to ring the lab earlier, as requested?"

He slapped his hands over his eyes and groaned. "Shit, I knew there was something else I had to do, boss. I suppose I got distracted with the information I was collecting and it slipped my mind." He reached for the phone on his desk. "I'll do it right away."

"No, you won't, I will. Carry on, folks. I'll have a chat with the pathologist, and then we'll have an open discussion about the information we've gathered so far." Sally picked up her mug and carried it into her office. She sat behind her desk and glanced at the cloudless blue sky, envious of those who were able to have outdoor jobs and weren't stuck inside every day.

Daft mare, I've only just come back. Granted, I was in and out of houses all morning and mostly driving around in my car, but at least I felt some rays on my face.

She dialled the number of the lab. One of the male technicians answered the call and told her that Pauline would ring her back within ten minutes as she was in the process of finishing off a PM, not related to her investigation. Sally sat there, waiting, tapping her pen on the desk. After boredom hit the next level, she picked up her mobile and called Simon. "Hey, you, it's me. Can you talk?"

"For five minutes. We're waiting for the estate agent to show her face."

"Likewise, I mean I've only got five minutes. I'm awaiting a call back from Pauline, the new pathologist."

He laughed. "I'm well aware who Pauline is."

"Sorry, my mind is in some kind of vortex this afternoon."

"How come? Do you need to chat about it?"

"Not really, it's all in hand. I'll fill you in when I get home tonight. I needed to hear your voice and know that everything was going well with you today."

"It is. Another project finished. Tony is going around making a snagging list now."

"Is this the property that was vandalised a few months ago?"

"No, that one sold last week. This is the house we made into three one-bedroom flats."

"Amazing. Bloody hell, I can't keep up with you. I'm so proud of what you've achieved since you changed careers, love."

"Hey, I'm surrounded by equally professional people. It truly makes a difference, I can tell you."

"Nevertheless, it's your initial funds and idea input that gets things underway in the first place."

"I'll give you that one. Hey, I detect you're a bit down

despite the praise you're dishing out. Do you want to discuss it?"

"No... umm... it's just that during the investigation today someone accused me of not knowing what it was like living through a domestic violence situation and..."

"You told them the truth, and now vile images of that arsehole are taking a toll on your mind, am I right?"

"I love you so much. Nothing gets past you."

"Not where you're concerned, darling. You know how much you mean to me. We're soulmates. Forget what has gone on before, you know it will never happen in the future, not with me. I could never hurt you, intentionally or otherwise."

"I know and I appreciate that, sweetheart. The mind plays funny tricks on you now and again, that's all."

"It will if you allow it. The key is to block out the images that you have locked away in that beautiful mind of yours. Maybe working with a hypnotist or some kind of therapist is the answer. We could discuss it over dinner tonight. I thought I'd create a new creamy chicken pasta dish."

"Sounds delicious." The phone rang on her desk. "Gotta fly, love you." She blew a kiss down the line and ended the call on her mobile while grabbing the landline. "DI Sally Parker, how may I help?"

"You wanted me?"

"I did, Pauline. Thanks for getting back to me. Is it too soon for me to request an update?"

"Yes, but you're going to anyway, aren't you?"

"I am. We've already started going around in circles, and it's driving me crazy."

Pauline sighed and shuffled some papers on her desk which rustled down the line. "I'm sure we all have our crosses to bear at times, dear Inspector."

"Come on, Paul… damn you, give me something to go on."

"I believe I've done that already by telling you the gender. What has your digging concluded, if anything?"

"I wasn't going to tell you this but I have a suspicion I know who the victim is."

"What? And pray tell me why I'm only just hearing about this now."

"Because, like I've told you already, it has been a bugger of a day. Frustratingly, there's been nothing concrete to hang on to, and I also feel we've been going round and round in circles."

"As you're inclined to do in such cases. I'm afraid I can't wave a magic wand and give you what you need at this stage of the investigation. However, I'm more than a little put out that you haven't felt the need to confide in me. This is not the type of relationship we agreed to, unless I'm wrong. Am I?"

"No, I apologise. Things have only just slotted into place this afternoon. As I've said, more than once, we've been chasing our tails. I'm also conscious about being extra cautious. If I supply the name we suspect, you might take your foot off the pedal."

"What the fuck are you saying? You clearly don't know me as well as you believe you do. I'll have you know that I'm an utter professional. I would never take someone's best guess and dismiss the hours and hours of work my forensic team and I have already thrown at the case. Just to make you aware, we're supposed to work together on an investigation. On the other hand, if you want to go down a different route to me, fair enough, but don't expect me to feel sorry for you when things backfire and you end up with a shitload of egg on your pretty face."

"All right, that's me told. Can we start afresh? I'll give you what I have and scrub past the mistake I've made in not keeping you informed."

"Whatever. Get on with it then, some of us have work literally coming out of every conceivable orifice."

Sally grinned. Relieved that she hadn't lost Pauline's trust, despite her unintentional screw-up. "Okay, this is what we've learned today. A Paul Coppell, who was a serious wife abuser, left the family home in two thousand, and neither his wife nor his two grown-up children have heard a single word from him since."

"And who was he? Or did you deliberately brush over the most important element?"

"He was a previous owner of number four."

"Hmm… okay. In that case, maybe keep going the way you are for now as the tech boys have concluded the body was buried under number six, not four."

"What? And you held back from sharing that snippet of information with me?"

"Not really. I only got word about it within the last hour. I was carrying out a PM at the time, and as you know, I was still in theatre up until a few minutes ago. I would have got around to telling you… eventually."

"Gee, thanks for pulling me up on not sharing information when you've done it yourself." *Hypocrite!*

"Oh, get off your high horse, Missy, and deal with the situation for what it is. I refuse to share information the very second I receive it, not with you or anyone else for that matter. I'm my own person and I work a case methodically, and there will be days when things get in the way, such as today, that being yet another PM. Have I made myself clear?"

"Perfectly clear. In my defence, I'm the one out there, pounding the streets, trying to ascertain who a victim is and how the damn crime was committed. Again, we need to work together if we're going to achieve great results in record time, meaning that we deal with cases effectively and efficiently."

"You took the words out of my mouth. It's a two-way thing, glad we've sorted that out."

A two-way thing? When it suits her! "But have we? Where do we go from here? When will we get a precise identification for the victim, if ever?"

"This morning I spoke to the anthropologist. She's agreed to work with me to reconstruct the face. What we can do in the meantime is everything we can to rule out the person who was reported missing. Who's to say it's not still him just because the remains were found next door?"

"I asked the family if Paul Coppell had left any belongings. They told me they had burnt every last scrap of his possessions because they couldn't wait to get rid of them."

"I see, that's not going to help then. In that case, all we have left open to us is mitochondrial DNA. We can obtain that from the bones and the teeth of the victim and match it to any living relatives. I believe you said he had children, am I right?"

"That's correct, two girls. I can't see there being any objections."

"Tough if there is. Do the necessary for me, and we'll do our bit at this end."

"Can you lend a hand on that one? Ask for the samples? Or show up out of the blue perhaps?"

"Me personally? Out of the question. What I can do is send a member of my team to gather the samples we need to make the comparison. Why the apprehension on your part?"

"There isn't, not really. All I'm trying to do is not intrude on the family's lives too much. The mother is going through chemo for cancer, and when we were there earlier, things got a little tetchy, shall we say."

"Ah, I hear you. You're going to need to rise above it and

get on with the investigation all the same, Sally. If you step on their toes then it's tough shit."

"Your lack of compassion and empathy is noted."

"Bollocks. Give me the address, and I'll get one of the techs out there to see them ASAP."

"I'll give you the eldest daughter's contact details, she's the one who appears to be in charge. Probably protecting her mother during her treatment."

"I believe I would be reacting the same way, wouldn't you? If we were talking about your mother dealing with cancer?"

"Okay, you've got me there. Do you want me to forewarn her that a member of the team will be getting in touch with her soon?"

"Yes, anything to make our lives easier."

"Okay, I'll do it now. How long before your anthro gets on with the job?"

"She's planning to start tomorrow, she's fitting it in as a favour to me and will be working on it for a few hours each evening after work, therefore, the whole process might take her weeks to complete."

"Shit! Not what I was hoping to hear."

"Regrettably, this is the real world, not a TV detective show where things manage to get solved overnight."

"I don't need to be reminded of that, thanks. I'll tell Paige that a member of your team will be in touch within the next day or two, how's that?"

"Perfect. Speak soon, and keep in touch if and when you uncover any evidence."

"I try to do just that with the pathologists I work with." Brushing aside the recent spat they'd had to the contrary.

"Or end up marrying, eh?"

"Get out of here. Our working lives and personal lives

were always kept separate. He was never one to make exceptions on that front, I can assure you."

"He wore two hats then… at all times?"

"Correct. Too right he bloody did, and I wouldn't have had it any other way. It was a decision we made early on in our relationship, our personal relationship, I should say."

"Ever the professional. Right, I can't hang around here talking to you all day. I have bodies to cut open and samples to chase up, you know how it is."

"Only too well. Thanks for getting back to me so quickly. I'll give Paige a call now, to prewarn her."

"You do that. Good luck and keep in touch. Sharing is caring, remember that. It will also ensure that the investigation gets solved quicker if we work as a team."

"Couldn't have said it better myself." Sally ended the call and immediately rang Paige who answered the phone after a few seconds.

"Hello, Paige Warren."

"Paige, it's DI Sally Parker, we met earlier."

"Yes, Inspector. What can I do for you?"

"I've just had a call from the pathologist. She wants to carry out further tests on the remains. I mentioned that your father had gone missing and we've agreed to try to rule him out by comparing your DNA with that of the deceased. If you're agreeable?"

There was a long pause on the other end. Sally wondered if Paige was even still on the line until she sighed and said, "If we must, but I'm telling you, my father went off and left us. He was a very selfish person. The type who impacted someone's life and then did anything and everything to disrupt it. Him leaving the way he did had a resounding impact on my mother. I believe he would have been elsewhere, rejoicing in the knowledge that we were all still living on the edge, expecting him to show his face one day in the future. I'm thrilled Mum got back out there and hooked up with Chris. He's been more of a father to me than the other one ever has."

"I'm glad. It must have been awful for you and Erica to have grown up in such a toxic environment."

"I can tell you it was never a bed of roses."

Paige fell silent. "Are you still there, Paige? There are people you and your sister can speak to if it's still affecting you today."

"It's not. I don't know where you get that impression from. We haven't spoken about him in years. We've led happy lives, all of us, and then to suddenly be confronted by you today with the news... well, it's bound to affect us, isn't it?"

"I suppose so. Anyway, I have to get on now. I wanted to forewarn you that someone from the lab will be contacting you within the next couple of days. The sooner we can carry out the necessary tests the quicker we're likely to obtain the results, if only to dismiss your father as being the victim."

"Whatever. It's not him, though. He left us, walked away, a gutless, selfish individual with absolutely no thoughts for anyone else, family or otherwise."

"Okay. I get the picture. I'll let you get on. I'll be in touch soon."

"You do that," Paige replied and ended the call.

Paige and her reaction remained with Sally. She left the office to share the news with the rest of the team.

"Listen up, folks. I spoke to the pathologist. She's confirmed that the body was buried at number six."

Lorne inclined her head. "What does that mean? That we're barking up the wrong tree where Coppell is concerned?"

"Possibly. She also told me that an anthropologist is going to embark on reconstructing the deceased's face. Plus, she

119

wants to compare the DNA samples with other members of the family."

"The daughters?" Lorne asked.

"Correct."

"That's going to go down well with them."

Sally shrugged. "If they object then we'll have reason to suspect they know more than they're letting on. I rang Paige, told her a tech bod will be sourcing samples of DNA from her and Erica, she seemed okay about it."

Lorne cocked an eyebrow. "Really? You do surprise me. I thought she would kick up a fuss."

"We'll see what happens when the time comes."

"What's the next step for us?" Lorne picked up her cup and took a sip. "Did you want one?"

"No, I'm fine. I want to go over what we've uncovered so far. Note down all the details that don't sit well with me, that sort of thing, and I think we should continue digging. Ouch, bad choice of words."

Lorne smiled. "And tomorrow?"

"Has anyone checked if the factory is still up and running? Simmons' Steels, another fact I forgot to share upon our return. Sorry, guys."

"Yes, I came up with two possible factories, and that was one of them," Joanna said.

"Okay, I think we should steer clear of there today and Lorne and I will pay them a visit first thing in the morning. Joanna, if you can get me the lowdown on the company. The usual, how long it's been going and who owns or runs it. That'll save us getting worked up about things in the morning before we leave."

"I've made a start already, boss."

"Great." Sally walked over to the whiteboard and was pleased to see Lorne had brought it up to date in her absence.

Lorne joined her.

"Thanks for this. Not something Jack would have considered doing. I appreciate you being my partner more than you will ever realise."

"Don't be silly. It's what I would have expected from my partner if I was carrying out duties elsewhere."

"You're a godsend all the same."

"We're from the same mould."

Sally's gaze ran the length and breadth of the board. "What are we missing?"

Lorne faced her. "I'm lost. What makes you say that?"

"There's something niggling me. We've spoken to all the neighbours now." Sally clicked her finger and forefinger together. "Maybe not all of them. The Evanses, do we know where they are?"

"I'm still trying to trace them, boss," Jordan shouted from the other side of the room. "When they sold the house, they moved into temporary accommodation for a while, and I haven't managed to find their whereabouts since."

"What about relatives?"

"I can look into that if you want me to," Lorne said.

"It makes sense to try and find them, considering that's where the pathologist believes the body was found."

"Let me see what I can find out."

"It's been a long day for all of us, and we've accomplished a lot so far, so no stress from me. We'll leave at five-thirty at the latest and start over again tomorrow. I don't know about you, but my brain is frazzled. We've had to have our wits about us today."

"I'm with you on that one," Lorne agreed.

CHAPTER 5

*S*ally had a restless night and decided to skip breakfast and get on the road early, much to Simon's disgust. He had prepared a sumptuous feast for them to set them both up for the long day ahead and was disgruntled when she turned him down flat.

It was rare for them to fall out. Sally took Dex for a reasonably long walk down by the river instead, to clear her mind, then headed off.

Now that Wymondham Station could be seen on the horizon ahead, she was none the wiser how to tackle the day. What if the body turned out not to be Coppell? Carrying out all this work would have been for nothing. What if he'd moved away, started afresh with someone else and even changed his name? The chances of finding him were virtually zilch. What was the likelihood of the factory boss being able to give her any further information?

"You look lost in thought." Lorne strolled into the office behind her.

Sally was at the drinks station, fixing herself her first cup of stimulant for the day. "Do you want one?"

"Have you ever known me to turn a coffee down?"

"Nope. Crap, this bloody investigation has got under my skin. I barely slept a wink last night."

"What's the point in letting it get to you? All we can do is our best. Uncover the facts and see where they lead us."

"If only it were that simple."

Lorne shook her head. "Christ on a pogo stick, this is only the second full day of the investigation. Give yourself a break, woman."

Sally chuckled and poured milk into a second cup, added sugar, a spoonful of coffee and hot water then handed it to her partner. "I can always depend on you to kick me up the arse."

Lorne winked. "I'll never let you down in that respect."

They both laughed, and the rest of the team wandered in to join them. Sally left Lorne making coffee for the new arrivals, and she drifted into her office to check what mind-numbing post was vying for her attention. Thankfully, there wasn't much, and she dealt with it before her coffee had a chance to go cold. Task completed, she collected Lorne, and they got on the road at a little after nine-thirty.

"Hopefully this won't take us too long to deal with," Sally said en route.

"And what if it does?"

"We'll handle it. I'm expecting the boss, if it's the same one still in charge, to be more than a little miffed."

"As long as he doesn't tell us to do one, we should be all right."

"Only time will tell."

They drove through the open countryside, the warm rays of the summer sun flooding the car.

Sally lowered her window and sucked in some fresh air. "It's days like this that I would love it if the world came to a complete standstill."

"Me, too. I can see us both standing in the middle of a field, arms out to the side, spinning on the spot, enjoying the wonders of nature surrounding us. I have to say, with that image set in my mind, I don't miss the Big Smoke one iota."

"Was it hard for you to adjust? I don't think I've ever asked you that since you arrived."

"No, I felt at home right away. It would have been lovely for Tony and I to have had the opportunity to get out there and explore the area more, but the dogs were our priority at the time, them and getting the house up to scratch. Then I joined the team and now I'm working harder than ever."

Sally screwed her nose up. "Now I know you're fibbing. You can't tell me this is work, not compared to working for the Met."

"Granted. I was winding you up. It's definitely a different pace of life up here, one that I'm relishing and don't intend changing anytime in the future. My only regret is…"

Silence filled the car.

"Go on, don't stop there."

"My only regret is that Charlie isn't here to enjoy it all with us."

"That would be ideal, but she's got her own life to lead, Lorne, it's something all parents have to accept when their children grow up."

"I know. I suppose I've been guilty of wrapping her in cotton wool most of her life, and to suddenly have that responsibility stripped away from me…"

"I get it. Even when she joined the Met she still lived at home with you until you made the move up here, didn't she?"

"She did, then she moved in with her fella and they split up, and I wasn't around to help her pick up the pieces."

"What are you saying? That you believe she's struggling down in London?"

Lorne turned her way, and her eyes widened. "Good grief,

no, not in the slightest. Don't ever let her hear you say that, either. Forget I said anything. Call it the nonsensical ramblings of a menopausal woman with regrets."

"Bless you."

"Apparently, hormones are complicated buggers to sort out."

"No news there then. I suppose every woman is built differently and it takes the medical profession a while to figure out what mixture of patches and tablets work for each individual. I'm glad it appears to be working out for you now. I bet Tony is relieved, too."

"Cheeky. He's always understood me. Even when I didn't really understand what was going on myself , he knew. He was the one who made the initial appointment with the doctor for me."

"He's amazing. Hard to imagine him being a devout bachelor before you came along. You were made for each other."

"A dream partnership as Charlie calls us. I'm not about to deny it."

"Like us, Simon and I. Except for this morning."

"Why? What happened?"

"I refused to eat breakfast. He was pissed at me because he'd cooked the works, fried bread, black pudding, the lot. I just couldn't stomach it after having a bad night. I took Dex for a walk instead and left the house without either of us saying goodbye."

"Oops. You should give him a call during the day, otherwise you're going to be in for a frosty reception when you get home this evening."

"I will, later. I don't know why my stomach is so churned up about this case. I can't remember dealing with such intense feelings before, ever."

"Are you sure about that? I bet that thought has crossed

your mind during every investigation you've ever worked on."

Sally shrugged, indicated and turned into the factory car park. "I can honestly say that simply isn't true. You used to tell me how you always relied on your gut instinct to solve a case, and I used to scoff at you. I'm getting the impression that this is something along those lines, except I can't put my finger on what's exactly is going on. I'm talking bloody gibberish now, aren't I? Go on, don't hold back."

"I won't. I'm not you, only you can figure out what is going on, Sally. All I can do is support you in the decisions you make throughout the investigation. I'll let you know if I think you're drifting off the path, if that's what you want?"

"Yes, do that. I'm giving you my permission to kick me up the jacksy, if and when it's needed, but only on this case. Haven't you ever felt this way, during an investigation?"

"Hard to say. I've been overwrought a few times during my career, mainly when members of my family have been targeted by the villains—not naming names, I'm sure you can guess who I'm talking about."

"Damn." Sally winced. "Why do I frigging do that? Insert my size fives in my mouth all the time?"

"You wouldn't be you if you didn't." Lorne laughed.

"Fuck off. And there was me appreciating how sympathetic you were being. It was all a bloody act, wasn't it?"

"No comment, in case I incriminate myself."

Sally parked the car at the rear, in the centre row, well away from the main entrance of the factory. "Seems to be a very busy place."

"It's been open for thirty-five years. Family-run business that has grown and grown. They had to diversify when the government put their spoke in and changed the regulations that caused several other steel companies to go under. I read they started making metal office equipment on a grand scale before any of the other firms followed suit. It turned out to be a critical decision for the company, and they made a killing. Their reputation grew tenfold and they've continued to listen and adapt to what was needed in the market ever since."

"That takes a lot of guts, especially if you're already a well-established company. Okay, here we go, let's see what we can find out."

The reception area was glass-fronted and furnished with comfy leather chairs with chrome legs.

"Blimey, this is a bit posh, innit?"

Lorne smiled. "Just a touch."

They both had their warrant cards handy and showed them to the smartly dressed blonde woman behind the enormous smoky-glass desk. The name plaque to her left said she was Sheila Francis.

"We're DI Sally Parker and DS Lorne Warner from the Norfolk Constabulary. We'd like a word with whoever is in charge around here. We know the company is a family-run concern."

"It is. I'll see if Mr Greg Simmons is available to speak with you. May I ask what it is about? He's bound to ask."

"It's regarding a matter which took place over twenty years ago. Was Mr Simmons in charge of the company around that time?"

"Yes. I believe he took over the reins from his father about twenty-five years ago."

"Good, then he's sure to know. I appreciate how busy he must be, running a very large factory. We shouldn't take up much of his time."

"Give me a few moments. Won't you take a seat?"

"Thanks, we'll stand while we wait."

"Very well," Sheila said. She tossed her hair over her shoulder and left her seat. She returned a few minutes later, beaming. "You're in luck, Greg is between calls and told me to tell you he can spare you five minutes. Any longer than that and you'll have to make an appointment to see him another time."

"Five minutes should suffice. Of course, that's dependent on the outcome of the meeting."

"I'd better take you to him. Time is of the essence around here these days."

"I'm sure."

She requested they follow her and knocked on the door close to the end of the hallway. A voice bellowed for her to enter. Pushing open the door, she announced, "DI Parker and DS Warner to see you, sir. Can I get you any refreshments?"

Sally smiled. "No, thanks, we're good."

"I've got some water here, should I need it, thanks, Sheila. Do come in, ladies, take a seat. Sheila told me your visit here today is regarding something that happened around twenty years ago, is that correct? If so, it seems a very long time in the past to be chasing up now. How can I help?"

Sally settled into her seat and then said, "We're making enquiries about a Mr Paul Coppell. Do you know him?"

Greg Simmons' eyes instantly narrowed, and he clenched his hands together on the desk in front of him. "I do. What's he done wrong?"

"It's more complicated than that. I'll give you a brief outline of what has prompted our visit to come and see you today."

He glanced at his watch and tapped the face. "Bearing in mind you only have five minutes to fill me in."

"It's okay, it shouldn't take long. A couple of days ago, we were called to a construction site where the remains of a body were discovered. We've spent the last forty-eight hours tracing all the former residents of the site. There were four cottages in total. There are still a few people we need to track down. One of them is Paul Coppell. We believe he used to work for this company around twenty years ago, is that correct?" Sally didn't have to be Einstein to work out that Simmons seemed furious when she'd voiced the name.

"He did. What do you need to know about him?" His tone became strained, and his back went rigid.

"Anything and everything you'd care to share with us would be a great insight and would also help our investigation. We've been led to believe he was a manager here, is that right?"

"He was. I trusted that man, and he let me down. I don't think I've ever recovered from the way he treated..."

Sally and Lorne shared a concerned glance, and Lorne withdrew her notebook and pen from her pocket.

"Go on," Sally urged. "Did he cause problems here? For you specifically, perhaps?"

"He single-handedly tarnished our reputation when we least expected it, during one of the most traumatic times in this company's history."

Sally frowned. "Care to enlighten us?"

He picked up his phone. "Bear with me while I make a call."

"Go right ahead."

"Sheila. Can you rearrange my schedule for the next thirty minutes and apologise to Frank and Ed for the inconvenience. I'm sure they'll understand." He ended the call and fidgeted in his seat. "Where do I begin? Let's put it this way, that man changed the way I view my staff."

"May I ask how?"

"He was a selfish individual who manipulated others for his own gain. At first, I wasn't prepared to believe the gossip, but the more I heard, the more I found it impossible to ignore."

He paused for a breath, and Sally jumped in to ask, "Gossip?"

"I'm coming to that, Inspector. If only I had been privy to the information months before he left, but alas, that wasn't the case. Although others will tell you differently."

"Sorry, you're not making any sense. Can you share with us what went on back in the day? You're aware that he went missing, I take it?"

"Yes, he just up and left, according to his family. When his wife rang me around that time, I remember speaking with her, furious, I was, while she came across as relieved. After all the revelations concerning him came to light, I totally understood why she was relieved."

"Revelations?" Sally prompted. She got the impression Greg was the type of man to embellish every story if he was getting someone's undivided attention. She'd come across a few men like him in the past.

"How shall I put this…? He was a sex pest. Had I known sooner, I would have dismissed him on the spot."

His gaze shifted to the left, telling Sally all she needed to know about his admission—it was a false one.

"And you had no idea what he was like whilst he worked for you?"

Again, Greg avoided all eye contact with her, and his gaze dropped to study his hands. "No."

"Were you aware of what his home life was like?"

His head rose, and their gazes locked. "Not until his wife rang to tell me the news. I couldn't believe what I was hearing. He disguised his character well. I never suspected a thing."

"Okay, when you said he was a sex pest, I take it he touched someone up at work."

His mouth twisted, and he licked his lips. "Several women, past and present employees at the time."

Sally frowned. "Past employees? You mean they left the company while he was working here as opposed to leaving after he went missing?"

"That's right."

"What were their reasons for leaving the firm?"

"Different reasons. I wouldn't be able to tell you off the top of my head."

"Would you mind checking for us? It's important we get all the facts."

He started to get out of his chair and then flopped back into it. "Wait, I need to ask what's really going on here. Why have you come here today? What's really behind your visit?"

"Laying our cards on the table. The body we found earlier this week might belong to Coppell, although we're awaiting the results of the post-mortem to corroborate that fact. In the meantime, we're doing all we can to build a picture of what the man was like and if he had any possible enemies who would want to kill him."

"Jesus! Really? Are you telling me he didn't take off and leave his wife then, as we all suspected at the time?"

"We can't say, not until we obtain a true identification for the deceased. All we can do for now is conduct the necessary background checks in case it's Coppell. I'm not really one who believes in coincidences. Him going missing only for his body to possibly show up twenty-odd years later... well, as I said previously, we're making general enquiries to see where that leads us. If you're telling us that he had a bad reputation then that is only going to strengthen our case against him. Adding a word of caution, we're still awaiting confirmation of the deceased's identity."

"From an outsider's point of view, it sounds to me like you've already made up your mind, Inspector."

Sally smiled. "My mind is always open until I have the evidence to back up such a claim, sir."

"I'll do anything I can to help you. What do you need? Although, having said that, if you discover anything untoward that went on around here in the past, I would very much appreciate you keeping it between us and not leaking it to the press."

"May I ask why? Not that I'm in the habit of leaking personal details about workers to the press."

"Times continue to be tough. I've seen firms ravaged by the written word over the years and I'd rather not have to deal with the fallout if it's all the same to you. I have shareholders to consider, all of whom are relatives of mine. What I'm trying to tell you is, they tend to come down heavily on me if things aren't running smoothly around here and, to be honest, I'm getting too old to deal with their shit. There, I've said it." He grinned, as if the revelation was a huge relief to him.

"You have my word that none of this will reach any journalist's hands. I never work that way. I have always preferred to play my cards close to my chest."

"Good to hear. Okay, I created a special file years ago with the evidence I had collected."

"Sounds intriguing. Would you mind sharing the details with us?" Sally smiled, trying to keep him onside, aware that time was against them and how long a warrant would take to obtain, if it came to the crunch.

"Let me see if I can locate it. I haven't laid eyes on it in years. There hasn't been any reason for me to revisit it, until today."

"We'd appreciate it."

He left his seat, and Sally nudged Lorne's leg. Lorne crossed her fingers, and Sally nodded.

"How long has the business been running, Greg?" Sally asked. Yes, Lorne had already given her that information in the car, but this was a test she often ran past someone, to see if they were being truthful or full of bullshit.

"It was started by my father and grandfather over thirty-five years ago. In fact, we celebrated the milestone a couple of months ago. Held a big party for the employees that went down well with everyone. We've always considered ourselves caring employers. That's why this undesired behaviour came as a bolt out of the blue." He collected a file that had been tucked at the back of the bottom drawer of the filing cabinet sitting in the corner of the room, and returned to his seat.

"I can understand. Is that it?" Sally asked what appeared to be an obvious question.

"It is. Let me flick through it, see if there are any secrets about the company that I need to remove."

"Fine by me. All we're interested in is if you have any complaints from staff members that we can chase up."

"There will be, I promise you. Give me a few moments."

After flipping through the pages, Greg slammed the file shut and slid it across the desk towards Sally. "Do with it what you will."

Sally's heart pounded. This could turn out to be the break they needed to get the investigation underway. Silence filled the room while she speed-read the file. "My God. I can't believe what I'm reading here."

She glanced up and noticed the colour rising up Greg's neck and finally settling in his cheeks. He didn't reply, simply hitched up his shoulders.

"Why believe him over the victims? Because he was a manager?"

"I suppose so. If you've never run a business, it's something we often have to deal with... that might be a gross exaggeration on my part. We have so many plates we're charged with spinning. Pressures we need to deal with every day."

"I don't understand what you're trying to say," Sally challenged.

"That sometimes, certain details come to your attention and you choose to brush them under the carpet rather than make a big deal out of it."

"So, let me get this right, you've just contradicted yourself. When this conversation began, you assured us you weren't aware of the allegations against Coppell, and now you're telling me that you chose to *ignore them* because they were an inconvenience. Please do correct me if my assumption is wrong."

"It's accurate enough and, believe me, I've had to live with the guilt for over twenty years. Like I said previously, this incident left a bitter taste in my mouth for months after Coppell did his disappearing act. That's when more and more women came out and accused him of either abusing them or sexually harassing them. My faith in human nature has been put in doubt ever since. I refuse to do any of the hiring and firing for the company because of how that man managed to pull the wool over my eyes. He set out to abuse his position. Often threatening the women involved, forcing them into an untenable situation. I was mortified. Back in the day, the doctor put me on tablets for my nerves, and I'm still taking them. But I don't want to make this all about me. The women are the ones who suffered at the hands of that despicable bastard, my sympathy has always been with them, but I've never been able to put my feelings across adequately enough."

"What? They felt that any sympathy you showed them as possibly insincere, is that what you're telling me?"

"I suppose that's what it amounts to, yes. If I could turn back the clock to before that man walked through the door for his first interview, I would, in a damn heartbeat. I can remember his first interview, he came across as a breath of fresh air compared to the other candidates for the position. My father sat in with me for the second interview, and he handed him the job there and then."

"You didn't consult one another before your father went over your head and offered him the job?"

"Nope, I didn't even have time to take a drag on my fag— we all smoked a lot in those days. And I definitely wasn't about to contradict my father's decision. I had far too much respect for him to consider ever doing that. I was stuck with Coppell, that's how I regarded the unfortunate position from the outset, however, over time he began working his magic on me. He was a real charmer at work. Ask any of the male colleagues who worked here at the time and they'll back me up and tell you that he was best buddies with all of them."

"It was only the women who had a problem with him, is that what you're telling us?"

He stared off into the distance and then lifted a finger in the air. "Actually, right before he went missing, I seem to recall Sid Parrish pinning him up against the wall one day in the canteen. I heard about it on the grapevine and when I demanded to know what the argument was about, they both stood their ground and refused to tell me."

"Is Sid still around?"

"No, he resigned not long after but before Coppell went missing."

"I don't suppose you still have his personnel file with his address, do you?"

He pointed at the manila folder in front of Sally. "I believe it should be in there, along with the details of the women Coppell assaulted. I made sure I kept everything in one place."

"Ah, right. Can I ask how many staff still work here from twenty years ago?"

"Only a few I can think of. Why?"

"I wondered if we could have a chat with them."

"I'd rather the staff weren't disrupted at this time, we're on a tight schedule to get a large order completed by the end of the week. Lots of overtime flying around, that sort of thing."

"Ah, I see. All right, we'll try and track down the staff in the folder first, and revisit the others in the future, if necessary."

"Sounds like a better option all round. Thank you for considering our business needs."

"Always happy to oblige when we can."

He peeked at his watch and smiled. "I'm sorry, I don't wish to appear rude, but I'm going to need to get back to work now."

"Of course, you've been more than accommodating."

Sally and Lorne left the office after shaking his hand and made their way back through the reception area out to the car.

"The plot thickens," Lorne said.

Sally opened her car door and rolled her eyes. "It sure does. Let's take a moment to go through the file and see who we can question. Coppell sounds like a real sweetheart and, judging by the number of names on his hit list, hated by many."

"And the suspect list keeps on growing."

"So it would appear. That always makes our job a tough one. But there's no point in us complaining about it."

"For the record, I wasn't. It was a statement of fact."

CHAPTER 6

$\mathcal{A}$s a stroke of luck, Carol Nash was at home when they showed up at her house. Sally introduced herself and Lorne and asked if she wouldn't mind going over a few details of what had happened when she'd worked at the factory.

Miss Nash appeared stunned, but her surprise instantly gave way to anger. "Yes, come in. I think it's about time I let go of all these pent-up feelings that have blighted my life for years."

She led the way into a large lounge with a cosy wood-burner stove in the fireplace. "Can I get either of you ladies a drink?"

"No, we're fine, thank you for the offer," Sally replied. "We're sorry to drop by unannounced like this, we took a gamble on you being at home."

"If you must know, I'm rarely out these days. I spend most of the time doing all I can to combat my nerves. I have agora-phobia and I'm prone to having anxiety attacks when I venture out. Rather than contend with all the hassle that entails, I tend to remain in my home."

"I'm sorry to hear that. Have you always suffered with it?"

"Oh no. I used to be a fairly outgoing person until... please, take a seat."

They all sat, Sally and Lorne on the sofa made of a vibrant blue fabric and Carol in the contrasting cream easy chair.

"Until?" Sally prompted.

"Until someone ruined my life."

"And that someone was?"

Carol stared at Sally and then shook her head. "I can't even bring myself to say his name. He destroyed my confidence, my life, my total existence as I knew it."

"Are we talking about Paul Coppell?"

Carol's eyes closed, and her whole body began trembling. Sally faced Lorne, fearful about what was going to happen next.

"Are you okay, Miss Nash... Carol?"

"I will be. Give me a moment to calm down. I'm working on my technique. I have certain things that trigger violent emotions within me, and he's one of them. It's because of him that my whole life got turned upside down."

"I'm sorry to hear that. The last thing I want to do is cause you any distress. Do you feel up to speaking with us about the time you spent at Simmons' Steels?"

Carol sucked in a couple of deep breaths and released them slowly. "I haven't thought about that person in years. Hearing his name has a devastating effect on my senses." The shaking returned. This time, only her hands seemed to be affected. "He put me through hell."

"Are you up to telling us what went on? The last thing we want to do is cause you any stress. On the other hand, this avenue of enquiries could prove vital to solving our investigation."

"Are you going to tell me why you're here? To show up after all these years, out of the blue to speak about *that man.*"

Sally revealed the reason behind them showing up at her door.

Carol gasped and slapped her hand over her mouth and remained like that for a few minutes, then her hand dropped into her lap and, wide-eyed, she asked, "Could it really be him?"

"There's every possibility, although we're being cautious not to come right out and say it."

Quietly, Carol said, "And I've been living on my nerves all this time, wondering if he would show up one day at my front door, and all the time he's been... dead. Damn, my life was ruined by him, and now I find out that he might have been dead all these years." She broke down in tears and buried her face in her hands.

Rocking back and forth, she sobbed and sobbed, and Sally and Lorne let her.

Eventually, with a large lump swelling in her throat, Sally took the decision to get closer to the woman and settled on the squishy arm of the chair. "Silly question coming up, are you all right, Carol? Do you need to take a moment to get yourself together?"

Carol glanced up, with tear-soaked eyes, she said, "No, I think I'll be fine. It's the shock of realising I've wasted so many years on someone so misogynistic only to find out he wasn't even around."

Sally raised a finger. "We need to be cautious, the body we found might not turn out to be his."

"Is that what you seriously think? Why come here, dredging up the past like this?"

"As I said, we're trying to form a picture of what he was like and what he got up to. If it is his remains that were uncovered then questions need to be asked as to how he was buried in concrete."

"I understand. Hey, as long as you don't think I'm capable

of doing that to him… killing him, is that why you're here today?"

"No, not at all."

"I'm not the one who finished him off, if it's him. Think about it, surely I would have been rejoicing in the fact he's no longer around rather than spending the past twenty years of my life dreading every single day from the minute I woke up. I've been living on the edge, not knowing if he would come knocking or how I would react if he did."

"I'm sorry you've put yourself through the torture and torment of living on your nerves."

"God, I don't know how I feel now, I'm not sure relieved is the word or not. There were reports, back in the day, that he went missing. I left the firm but remained friendly with a couple of girls who went through a similar ordeal to what I'd been through. They didn't allow their emotions and state of mind to get in the way of going on to live happy lives, knowing he wasn't around. I couldn't get past it, he utterly and unequivocally destroyed my life."

"Can you tell me what he did? Or wouldn't you be able to live through the trauma again?"

"I relive that day over and over in my head, at least twenty to thirty times a day, often through the night as well, when sleep evades me, which it frequently does. I had only been at the company three months. I thought I was getting on well with everyone, the men and women alike."

"What job did you do?"

"I was a secretary. I worked in one of the smaller offices being a junior member of staff. Everyone had their place, and mine was in a cubby-hole of an office which was situated between two managers. I worked for both of them on occasion, but in the main I was what they called a 'utility secretary'. I got my head down, loved the job, and after three months I thought I had settled in quite well. I hadn't fallen out with anyone, ticked any of the other secretaries off with my level of efficiency—sometimes that could cause a rift at work between the staff. No, I got on with my job and left work every night at five minutes past five."

She paused to take a breath. Sally, sensing that Carol was coping much better, returned to her seat.

"What did he do, Carol?"

"It happened on a Friday night. Some of the girls had invited me to go for a drink after work. I agreed, even though I was nervous about attending the session. At the time, I was the type who would colour up if someone said more than a few words to me. I suppose you'd call it lacking in self-confidence. Although I carried out my duties efficiently and thoroughly, I wasn't very good at interacting with other people."

"That's a shame, and what? He saw that as a weakness in you?"

"I can only presume that to be the case. I was in the process of tidying my desk before I headed over the road to the pub for the end-of-week bash. I remember putting some files away in the cabinet and turning round to find him behind me. I gasped, and he grinned. It was as though he revelled in the fact that he'd scared the shit out of me. He asked if I was going to join the others at the pub. I replied that was my intention. He grinned again and took a step towards me. If I'd had the space to do it, I would have retreated, but I didn't. Then he pounced... covered my lips with his." Her eyes squeezed shut, and sweat broke out on her forehead.

Sally reached over and patted a hand on Carol's knee. "Take your time, we're in no rush."

"He was such a vile man. He came across as everyone's best friend, but the second you were trapped inside a room with him... I can only describe him as a Jekyll-and-Hydetype character. The way his eyes blazed, his gaze penetrating every pore of my skin." She shuddered and then drew in several more breaths to calm herself.

"Take your time," Sally repeated.

"He was evil, pure evil, but no one could see it. It was as though he wore a mask at work, afraid to reveal his true identity. I heard later that his wife and girls suffered from abuse. I don't know how accurate those reports were, but I can totally believe it after what he did to me."

"We saw them yesterday and can confirm that's true."

"I knew it. You could see it in his eyes how much he detested women. Only needed them... you know, for his own sexual gratification."

Sally nodded. "I know, that type of man should never be allowed to walk the earth. I speak from experience, I can assure you."

"What?"

Sally waved a hand. "My ex-husband was created from the same mould. They live amongst us. Total charmers until it comes to the crunch."

"No, you're a copper and didn't suspect anything?"

"I am, and no, not until it was too late. But getting back to what happened to you that night, if you're able to walk us through the events as they unfolded."

"He pounced on me. His hands roaming my body, not gently either. There was an urgency there that was loath-some. The second his hand went up my skirt... I knew I had to put up a fight to prevent the inevitable from happening."

She paused again.

Sally allowed her to take the break to complete her tale. "There's truly no rush."

"No, I want to rid myself of the awful images that have plagued me half my life. If he is dead, then maybe my healing can now begin. Retelling the incident might help to rid me of the nightmare images that punish me every day."

"Go for it, I think it will help ease the pain."

"I kicked out at him and kneed him in the crotch. He bent over in pain. Shocked, he stared at me, but then I noticed his eyes narrow, and he came at me again. His strength had increased to another level. I struggled to fight him off a second time. He was too strong, too powerful, and my willingness to put up a fight dwindled quickly. He kicked my legs from beneath me and slapped a hand over my mouth to prevent me from screaming. In the hallway, I could hear my work colleagues laughing, heading to the pub. My door was closed. Had he left it ajar, I think one of them would have stuck their head into the room to see if I was ready to join them. At least I think that's what would have happened. I'm sorry it didn't… just by them checking in on me, that nightmare could have been avoided. As it was, I got the impression he felt empowered. By this time, he was sitting on top of me, his legs on my arms, preventing me from moving beneath him. His hand still over my mouth. I tried to wriggle free, but his strength overwhelmed me."

"It's okay. Take a break when you need one. Can I get you a drink?"

Carol reached down beside her and picked up a bottle of water. She took a long swig and replaced it on the floor. "I can still remember the emotions welling up inside me on that day. The fear, the anguish. I was too petrified to move. His hand held firmly over my mouth. Even if I had summoned up the courage to scream, it would have been suppressed." Again, she closed her eyes. Small droplets of tears slipped from her eyes. She wiped them away with the backs of her hands.

Even though she was putting herself through the nightmare again, as Sally had needed to all those years ago after

Darryl had raped her, she knew the strength that would emerge in Carol once this particular ordeal was over. It wasn't the most pleasant experience in the world but a necessary one for a woman to go through in order to heal herself from within.

"I'm so sorry," Carol said. "You haven't come here to watch me fall apart."

"Look, if that's what it takes for you to heal, then go right ahead. We're here to support you."

"I've never dealt with the memories head-on like this before. I've only ever reached halfway and then backed off."

"Take another breath, it'll help rid you of the toxins building up inside."

She did as instructed and then sat forward and closed her eyes. This time, she found the courage to complete her story. "I'll never forget his strength. I've never really considered myself a weak person, not really. I used to help my dad chop wood on the farm when I was a child and move large bales of straw when the tractor occasionally broke down. But that day, he knew exactly how to pin me to the ground, to combat any willingness in me to put up a fight. As if the move was well practiced. Perhaps he raped his wife and kids a lot, I don't know, that's me probably talking bullshit. It went on for ages, him fumbling with my clothes, making sure he had access to... you know what. I hated him at that moment. An all-consuming hatred for the despicable man. Eventually, he did what he had to do and let me go. I lay there, frozen to the spot, him staring down at me. He laughed and said it wouldn't be the last time he laid his hands on me."

"Then what happened?" Sally asked, a cold chill descending despite the high temperature outside.

"I waited until he left and lay there, disgusted with myself for allowing him to take advantage of me. I've hated myself ever since. I know none of it was my fault, but not having the strength or the willpower to fight him off will live with me forever."

"Have you ever thought about counselling? It truly helps. I believe everyone who has suffered an assault should bite the bullet and seek help from a professional."

"Did you?"

"Yes, eventually. It healed the wounds, I promise you. But most of all, it made me realise that none of it was my fault. He was in the wrong, not me."

"I'm not sure. Maybe I'll have the courage to seek advice now that I've revealed the truth to you."

"Do it. I'll be there to support you, should you need it."

Carol's gaze fixed on Sally's. "Thank you, that means everything to me. I haven't got any family members I can count on. I lost both my parents a few years after the incident occurred. They were aware of what went on. I swear it killed my mother. My father was so enraged, he went to his house, but it was too late, he'd already gone. I couldn't bring myself to tell them the truth until I left the firm a few weeks or a month later."

"Did you raise a complaint with the owners while you were there?" Sally tried to recall what it said alongside Carol's name in the file.

"What was the point? He was a manager. They wouldn't have believed a newcomer, would they? Although I did mention the reason I was leaving in my resignation letter. Greg Simmons called me into his office on my final day and asked me for my account of the incident. I stumbled, couldn't go into detail. I'd found another job elsewhere, and that was all that mattered to me. To move on. Except I couldn't. When I started my next job, I couldn't help looking at my male colleagues differently. Aware of the masks some men hid behind. The boss called me into his office one day. I remained by the door the whole time, refused to take a step closer or sit down. He found that behaviour inappropriate and unacceptable and fired me that week."

"Damn, couldn't you have told him the truth?" Sally asked.

"I don't think he would have believed me. I went on to try another couple of jobs after that, but the thought of being trapped inside an office, alone with a man, absolutely freaked me out. Depression set in soon after I left my fourth role in as many months, and I've since been unable to leave the house much. All because of what that disgusting pig did to me. He ruined my life, and if the remains do belong to him... then all I can say is good riddance and may he burn in Hell. Vile men like that don't deserve to share the same air as the women they set out to assault."

"I wholeheartedly agree. I promise you, now that you've taken the first step in opening up, you'll see that you've turned a corner. My advice would always be for someone in your position to seek help from the medical profession. It's imperative that you rid yourself of the memories that keep emerging, afflicting your days and nights. Someone needs to impress upon you that the gravest mistake was made by the person who attacked you, it had nothing to do with your inability to fend off the aggressor. I can't emphasise that enough."

"Knowing how I feel now, just airing my experience with you two ladies, I think I have gathered enough confidence to seek out the help you're talking about. I hope so, anyway."

Sally handed Carol one of her cards. "Let me know how you get on. Call me if I can be of any further assistance in that department."

"Thank you. This is you going the extra mile because you were once in my shoes, isn't it?"

"Partially, yes. I have a motto that I live by, too, one that everyone should take on board."

146

"Which is?"

"'Don't let the bastards grind you down'. I have a second one as well: 'what doesn't kill you makes you stronger'."

"I like you, Inspector. I can see the determination in your eyes. You coming here to chat with me today will give me the strength to continue."

Sally and Lorne stood.

"I'm glad to hear it. Get out there, make something of your life. Don't let the memories ruin what lies ahead of you. It's true what they say, 'The world really is your oyster', and it's there for the taking, if you want it."

Carol got to her feet and surprised Sally by giving her a hug. "I can't thank you enough. I hope you manage to solve the riddle as to whom the remains belong and why they were buried. I've already aired my feelings if it turns out to be him but, believe me, you needn't look in my direction searching for the culprit. I wouldn't have it in me to take another person's life, no matter how far I'm pushed."

Sally smiled and touched Carol's arm when they came to a standstill at the front door. "I believe you. Don't forget to contact me once you've made your first appointment with a counsellor. I meant what I said about supporting you."

"I'll do that. Thanks again."

They left the house and returned to the car.

Inside, Lorne sighed. "What a terrible shame that one incident has ruined her entire life."

"It sickens me. It also shows me how determined and resilient I was dealing with my ex. If it hadn't been for the team surrounding me and for my parents taking me under their wings the way they did, I wouldn't be the person I am today. I could easily have turned out like Carol."

Lorne vigorously shook her head. "There's no way. You're stronger than that, always have been, Sally."

"That's debatable. Anyway, it doesn't matter, it's in the

past now. It's all coming out about Coppell, what a bastard he was."

"Yep, it also means that the suspect list is growing, if it's him."

"I don't think there's any doubt in my mind any longer, what about you?"

"I'm of the same opinion, but until Pauline verifies it, I think we still need to be cautious."

"Absolutely. Right, on to the next one. We struck lucky with Carol being at home. I think I'll give the next lady a call in case she's at work or out shopping." Sally flipped open her notebook and ran her finger down the list of names. "Here we are, Julie Stevenson. I'll give her mobile a call." She dialled the number, and an abrupt voice answered. "Hello, is this Julie Stevenson?"

"Yeah, who wants to know?"

"Hi, Julie, I'm DI Sally Parker from the Norfolk Constabulary. I'd like to drop by and have a chat with you, if it's possible?"

"Police? Why? What have I done?"

"Nothing, as far as I know. We're making enquiries into an investigation we're working on."

"You're going to need to give me more than that."

"We'll fill you in when we get there. Are you at home?"

"As it happens, it's my day off. Do you have the address?"

"Twenty-four Charter Road, Hingham, is that your current address?"

"That's right. How long are you going to be?"

"About fifteen minutes, if that's okay with you?"

"It's going to have to be. I've got to pick up my granddaughter from school later, my daughter is away on a work course for the day."

"We shouldn't keep you too long. See you soon."

"I'll be here."

. . .

THE HOUSE WAS RUN-DOWN COMPARED to the neighbours on either side, but the small front garden looked newly created judging by the size of the plants in the beds.

Julie Stevenson was a plump woman with short greying hair. She welcomed them at the front door and invited them into the kitchen and gestured for them to sit at the kitchen table, which was clear except for the condiments sitting in the middle.

"Right, what's this about? I'd prefer it if you got to the point and didn't dilly-dally."

"It's concerning something that happened at Simmons' Steels around twenty years ago."

Julie rolled her eyes. "I bet I can guess what that was. The assault I reported, am I right?"

"That's correct. Would you mind going over the details of the assault with us?"

"Not until you tell me why. Why drag this up after all these years? Has something else gone on at that bloody factory, something along the same lines?"

"No, not as far as we're aware. We're chasing up a lead we have regarding our investigation."

"I get that. What bloody investigation? Come on, tell me or get out." Her tone instantly changed from abrupt to angry.

"Very well. A few days ago we were called to investigate the remains of a body that were discovered at a construction site."

Julie frowned and ran a hand around her face. "A body? And pray, what the fuck does this have to do with me and the debacle that happened around twenty years ago?"

"We're making enquiries because there's a possibility that the remains belong to Paul Coppell."

Julie's eyes flew open, and she shook her head. "Jesus, I

149

really never thought I'd hear that damn name again. If it is him, then good, I'll be sure to do a happy dance when you leave. The man was nothing more than the Devil incarnate. Effing evil to the core, that one."

"So we've been led to believe. All we're trying to do at this stage is form a picture of his character and try to ascertain what he got up to the few months leading up to his disappearance."

"That's right, I'd heard from one of the girls at the factory he'd gone missing. I thought it was strange at the time, but on the other hand, it didn't really surprise me."

"May I ask why?"

"Maybe he couldn't hack all the added pressure."

"Pressure? In what respect?" Sally asked.

"You know, once things started to escalate. The more women who spoke out about the filthy mongrel, well, it was bound to raise suspicions in the end."

"Ah, I see what you mean. Would you mind going over the details of what happened to you?"

She sighed and rolled her eyes again. "It's a good job I'm tough and not the type of woman who sits around and wallows in self-pity, not like Carol Nash. I don't mean that disrespectfully, but she should have got on with her life and refused to let the shithead get to her. Maybe I was able to brush things off because of my upbringing. I was brought up with three brothers, so I had a good foundation for dealing with men that stood me in good stead."

"I think everyone is different and it depends on the severity of the assault. Are you aware of what occurred with Carol?"

"I suppose you're right. Coppell hounded me for months, groped me mostly, until things went too far. I didn't mean to trounce over Carol's claims either. I'm sorry, she went through hell at the time. I guess what I'm trying to say is, look how she allowed it to affect her life, there was no need for that. Most women I know are stronger than she is. Why let the bastard keep winning all these years later?"

"While I agree with you, no one knows what tricks the mind plays on someone else. We're all built differently, some able to overcome trauma better than others. I don't think we should sit here and judge someone just because they're perceived to be weaker than us."

"I truly didn't mean to do that. I had this conversation with her years ago, tried to help her get past the trauma, but she was having none of it. Accused me of not understanding what was going on in her head. Too right I didn't. I told her to get some help, talk to someone if she was struggling that much. She refused to do that. In my opinion, she was keen on all the attention she received. Of course, I wouldn't say that to her face."

"I'm glad. Having recently interviewed Carol, I have to tell you that I didn't get that impression at all."

"Oh well, each to their own."

"Can you go through your experience with us?"

"What's to tell? I used to work on the shopfloor. He was a regular visitor to my area. Always brushing past me in confined spaces, you know that type of thing. One day, he asked me to stay behind to go over some production figures with him. I thought it was strange at the time that he didn't want to speak to my supervisor about that kind of shit. All I did was ensure the machines worked efficiently to take all the steel to the melting facility on the other side of the yard. As it was, he didn't consult with me on the subject at all, he clearly had his own agenda." She fell silent. Her nose wrinkled, and her eyes narrowed. She stared at the condiments on the table for a while and then ran a hand over her face. "Sorry, I didn't mean to drift off then. I was trying to recall the details I've successfully locked away for years. Unlike

others I could mention. We need to do that so we can
successfully carry on with our lives, don't we?"

"Always advisable. What do you recall about that day?"

"That he was getting closer to me, making me feel
uncomfortable because we were alone. I made an excuse to
go to the toilet. He seemed angry but allowed me to leave. I
took a moment to consider what my options were. They
were limited as you can imagine. I used one of the cubicles,
had a wee and, bugger me, when I came out, he was standing
there, arms folded, leaning against the bloody sink."

Sally's interest piqued. "Really? And this was a single-sex
toilet, I take it?"

"Too bloody right it was. I didn't know what to say, he
was my manager, and here he was, in the sodding ladies'
toilets with me. After all the attention he'd been giving me
outside, I feared there would only be one outcome. I geared
myself up for the fight, not that I had anything to hand to
defend myself with except my fists. So I used what I had at
my disposal when he advanced towards me. It was the look
in his eyes that I struggled with at the time. I swear they
changed colour from brown to a flaming red, it was only for
an instant, but it was there nonetheless. Evil fucking critter,
he was."

She paused, and Sally smiled.

"You're doing well, take your time."

"I'm okay, just doing what I can to give you the facts. It's
been a while since I revisited the scene in my head. I
wouldn't want to be accused of making up part of my story."

"In your own time, we're in no rush."

"You might not be, but I need to get to the supermarket
before I pick up my granddaughter from school."

Sally nodded. "I understand. Did he say anything to you
in the toilet?"

"Yeah, the smarmy fucking shit. He stood there, a smirk

on his face, telling me that he'd noticed the admiring glances I kept bloody giving him. I did nothing of the sort. If anything, I always gave him a wary look. I spent most of my time on guard. I am the same today with any man I've ever worked with since. In those days, I was stick thin and used to wear miniskirts a lot. A big fan of Mary Quant, I was, from a young age, right up to my early forties. That's when the weight started to pile on because I hit the menopause early. We always have to deal with some kind of shit going on with our bodies, don't we? Men are so damn lucky, they just breeze through this life with none of the hassles like having kids, experiencing the change. I keep saying, next time I'm hoping to come back with meat and two veg between my legs."

Sally and Lorne both laughed.

"They do seem to have an easy time of it compared to the female gender, you're right. However, it shouldn't have mattered if you wore miniskirts or not, not unless there was something in the rules where you worked to say otherwise."

"Some places are a bit fussy, but not many. This day I had on one of my shorter skirts. As soon as I saw him ogling me during his rounds first thing that morning, I regretted my choice of clothing that day. And here we were, alone in the ladies', with him coming towards me. His eyes changing colour, the intent etched into his features. I prepared myself, clenched my fists and hid them slightly behind my back so he didn't notice. His gaze ate through my skin. Caused me to shudder, it did. He probably misread the signs and thought I was excited about being there with him. That grin he used to have, I suppose I'd describe it as menacing, no other word for it really. He was vile with a capital V, I assure you. I was tempted to run back into the cubicle if only to vomit. I can remember the bile rising in my throat."

She swallowed and closed her eyes.

"It's okay, you're doing great, no pressure from us," Sally offered her the encouragement to reach the end of her tale. "What happened next?"

"I took a few steps back, hoping he would take the hint and back off himself. He did the complete opposite, he took it as a come-on and ran at me. I hit him, beat his chest with my clenched fists and shouted no. It made no difference, he was set on... punishing me, I suppose you'd call it. I didn't let up, though. Most women would have given in to him, his strength was unbelievable, but believe me, I was as determined as he was and put up a fight he hadn't expected. I lashed out with my fists and added a knee and a stomp of the foot here and there, too, for good measure. He seemed to revel in me putting up a fight, though, if that makes sense. I think any other man would have given up once I lumped him a few times, but not him. He kept coming, enjoying the contest of strength. Horrible man."

"Did he say anything during the fight?"

"Yes, a couple of times I heard him mumble that I was asking for it or I had asked for it for months. I'd done no such thing. I was happily married at the time, I never cheated on my husband. He cheated on me, but I didn't find out about that shit until our marriage had ended. That's by the by, Coppell shouldn't have been in the loos or coming at me. I felt trapped after a while, cornered. My back slammed up against the door of one of the cubicles, and I toppled back. It gave him the advantage. I landed on the toilet seat. While I was distracted during the fall, he pinned my arms above my head against the wall with one of his large hands and with the other, unzipped his trousers." She closed her eyes, just like Carol had, clearly sickened by the images filling her mind. "I'm sorry. I'm sure you know what came next. In the end, it would have been pointless trying to put up a fight, so I gave in. I never thought in a million years that I would ever do that, I regarded myself as one of life's fighters, however, he seized the opportunity and trapped me. When it was all over, he zipped up his trousers and walked away as if nothing had happened. I sat there, taking it all in, or trying to. A cloud of disbelief and disgust descended. I couldn't move, not for a while, and then I had to shift quickly, open the loo, and I vomited. I felt repulsed, knowing what that evil bastard had done to me. Furthermore, I knew that when it came time to leave the factory I would have to face him again. He was always on hand to lock up when the last member of staff left for the evening."

Sally sighed. "I'm so sorry you had to go through that horrendous ordeal."

Julie shrugged. "It's one of those devastating things that life sometimes hits you with."

"It needn't be, though. Men like that need to be locked up. Did you go to the police?"

"No, I couldn't bring myself to do it. Do your research. Rape cases weren't always dealt with by sympathetic officers back in the day."

"Something that I'm glad has been suitably addressed over the years."

"It's taken long enough. All the same, I still think the system is lacking."

"When you eventually surfaced, what did he do?"

"He annoyed the fuck out of me by bowing as I passed and said, 'Goodnight, Julie, the pleasure was all mine'. Fucking cretin. It still makes my skin crawl when I think about him. I haven't put myself through that for a long time."

"Sorry we've caused you to revisit your experience. What did you do next? I can't imagine you're the type to let him get away with it."

"Oh no. I mulled it over for a few days. In the meantime, I'd started picking up snippets of gossip about him touching up a few of the other girls. Then when Carol Nash left and one of the secretaries shared what they had seen in her resignation letter, my confidence grew and I ended up going to see Greg Simmons."

"Okay, and how did he react?"

"Not very well. He virtually called me a liar and ordered me out of his office. It took a lot of guts for me to go upstairs and see him, run the risk of bumping into Coppell while I was up there. It would have been obvious why I was visiting the owner of the factory, not many members of staff set foot in that area at all."

"Oh dear, so he never followed up on your complaint?"

"Not at all."

"I bet that made your working life untenable, didn't it?"

"You could say that. A few weeks later they fired me."

"What? Why?"

"They carried out a spot check on the lockers. Funny, we'd never heard of that before, and I'd worked there for over five years. I couldn't believe it when Coppell and another manager found large scraps of steel in my locker. I certainly hadn't put them there. I did my best to tell them that I'd been set up, but they weren't interested. The pair of them marched me upstairs, made me stand in front of Greg Simmons, and they revealed what they had found. I denied it, of course, but it fell on deaf ears. I was escorted off the premises there and then. I received no severance pay which I fought through a tribunal. I wasn't about to let them get away with that, the fuckers. They needed to realise they couldn't treat members of their staff like they were dollops of shit on their shoes."

"Did the managers have to give evidence at the tribunal? I'm not sure if that's the setup with one of those or not."

"No, they couldn't be bothered to show up. I believe that's what went against them in the end. I was awarded everything

I was owed in overtime, back pay, holiday pay for the rest of the year plus compensation for unlawful dismissal. Up until then, I'd had an exemplary record and had never received a warning, relating to my work. It was the undoing of any argument they put forward in their absence. Had I lost the case, then I would have gone after Coppell and submitted a rape claim with the police. My solicitor warned against that, though, because of the time that had elapsed."

"Fair point. It's always best to report a crime right after it has happened, especially in the case of rape. I'm glad you got compensated by the company."

"I only got what was rightfully mine. What I was entitled to. The whole couple of months left a bitter taste in my mouth. The bosses at that factory treat their workers like shit most days. It never used to be like that, not when old Mr Simmons was in charge. He realised the valuable role each member of staff had within the company, respected us equally. That all changed when his son took over. Shame on him for being such a coward. Had he been more forthright with the managers then Coppell wouldn't have been allowed to have got away with what he did, for months on end. Simmons is a typical bully, they both were, eager to lay the law down where women were concerned but were far more lenient when dealing with their male colleagues."

"Are you saying that you believe Greg Simmons was the same as Coppell? Or just saying that he chose to ignore Coppell's disrespectful and misogynistic behaviour?"

Julie shrugged and inhaled a large breath. "I'm not sure, you'll have to ask him that. He was easily led by Coppell, possibly manipulated into doing and saying things he might never have said or done off his own bat. Like fitting me up. Well, I had the last laugh on that one, didn't I?"

"You did. I'm glad you fought for your rights. Are you still in touch with anyone from your factory days?"

"I am. We go for a drink together once in a while. A couple of the women went through the same experience I had with Coppell. We do our best to avoid the subject when we go out, keen not to dwell on the vile bastard, but now and again, one of the women will feel a bit down and the tales would come pouring out."

Sally opened her notebook and picked out a couple of names. "Are these women Vera Bond and Alessia Kane?"

"That's right, amongst others."

"Others? Other women who were assaulted by Coppell?"

"Yes, after watching the consequences I suffered, some of them refused to speak up. But we all knew, it wasn't up to the ones who had spoken out to force the issue. They had their reasons for staying quiet."

"I should imagine it was a hard call to make."

"You need to speak with Alessia Kane next if you're going to speak to anyone. She's got a tale and a half to tell that is bound to curl your toes."

"Do you know what her current address is?" Sally asked, eager to see what this Alessia had to say for herself.

"It's thirty-two Belmont Road, over in Attleborough. Do you want me to give her a ring for you? To pave the way as it were?"

"No, it's fine. Do you know what shifts she works?"

"I think mainly mornings, she's part-time now, so you should catch her at home. Sometimes I'll pop over and see her for a coffee in the afternoon or meet up with her in town."

"Thanks for all your help."

"I'd say it has been a pleasure, but I'd be lying, having to revisit the most horrendous event in my life, and no, that's not an exaggeration. When do you think you'll find out who the body belongs to?"

"Hopefully soon, but procedures like this tend to take

time, as you can imagine. The experts are going all out to help us, which is a blessing."

She showed them to the door, said farewell and closed it behind her.

"I can't wait to find out what tale the next one has to share with us, if she confides in us," Lorne said on the way back to the car.

"Whatever it is, I think I'm past being shocked with this investigation. What a fucking scumbag he was, this Coppell fella."

"I'm not about to disagree with you. Men like that deserve to be buried in concrete. No one is going to mourn their loss, are they?"

"Maybe I should have thought about that and bumped Darryl off one night."

"Ah, but then you would have needed to have known someone who could pour concrete to have completed the job."

"True enough. I wonder if the team are any closer to finding the Evanses at number six. They have to be the key to solving this investigation, don't they? If, as we suspect, the body was found on their property."

"Let's just say, I'm more than a little intrigued to know how it got there. Want me to check in with the team?"

"Good idea. I'll set up the satnav and we'll get underway."

Both tasks were carried out efficiently with contradictory results. While Sally had success and started the journey feeling in a buoyant mood, Lorne put the dampener on it by ending her call with a disgruntled groan.

"Still nothing on the Evanses. Where the heck are they hiding? And is it deliberate? These are the questions we need answering, and soon."

"Never mind. We mustn't lose hope. Maybe we should ask the next couple of interviewees, see if they know where they are or where they moved to at the time. What do we know about him so far? Can you remind me?"

"They moved to Norwich as far as I can remember."

"What are the odds on finding them there? No, don't answer that, it was a rhetorical question."

"Glad about that because I wouldn't have a clue what to tell you."

"Onwards and upwards. Let's continue to be grateful for the hands we've been dealt during the case, so far."

"I agree. What's the point in worrying about aspects that are out of our control?"

CHAPTER 7

$\mathcal{T}$he bungalow in Attleborough was tiny and compact inside. Once Sally introduced herself to Alessia Kane, the welcoming smile slipped from her face.

"What's this about?" the older woman in her early fifties demanded. She leaned against the wall in the hallway and crossed her arms over the apron she was wearing.

"We're making general enquiries about a Paul Coppell, do you know him?"

Her eyes narrowed and bored into Sally's. "I'm guessing you already know the answer to that."

"I do. Are you up to speaking with us about him?"

"Do you want a cuppa?" she asked and spun on her heel to head up the hallway.

"Thank you. Two white coffees with one sugar."

Sally and Lorne followed her into the small kitchen at the rear of the property.

"It's a bit of a squeeze. Mind if I get on with rolling out my pastry? Dean loves his steak and kidney pie, although it has to be homemade, none of this shop-bought crap."

"You carry on. Would you like me to make the drinks, save you an extra job?"

"As you wish. Coffee is there on the side, along with the sugar, and the milk is in the fridge. Mugs are on the draining board. Help yourself."

Sally dried the mugs on a clean tea towel and threw together the drinks while the kettle was boiling. Alessia got back to rolling out her pastry on the marble board sitting on the worktop in front of her.

"Do you enjoy cooking?" Sally asked.

"I have to be in the mood to spend hours in the kitchen. My husband needs a compass to find his way around here, even if it's to make a pot of tea. Why are men so useless in the kitchen? Or is it only mine who falls into that category?"

"Speaking frankly, mine is better in the kitchen than I am. But my partner's husband is a bit like yours."

"He is," Lorne agreed. "Thankfully, his skills lie elsewhere, which suits me. He's a dab hand around the house. I suppose they can't all be good at everything."

"No, but some skills might come in handy," Alessia said. "My hubby is distinctly lacking in all departments."

Sally chuckled. "Sorry to hear that." She finished making the drinks and carried two mugs to the table and sat next to Lorne in the tight space around the circular table.

Alessia rolled out the pastry, turned it and rolled it again, then she placed it over an enamel pie tin that Sally had noticed was filled with a cold mixture of meat and onion. An upturned eggcup lay in the centre of the dish. Once Alessia had laid the pastry over the top, she made a few slits in the lid to let the steam out and pushed it to the back of the worktop then washed down the sides.

"There, that didn't take as long as I anticipated. Obviously one of those days when things decided to go well." She took a seat at the table and clenched her hands. "Now, how can I help you?"

"As I said before, we're making enquiries into Paul Coppell, or more to the point, his disappearance back in two thousand."

"Jesus, that's a name from the past I never thought I'd hear again. Why? Has something come to light after all these years?"

"Several things actually. I'll fill you in on how this investigation began."

Alessia listened with interest as Sally revealed the events of what had occurred at the beginning of the week.

"Jesus, and what are you saying? That you believe the body is his? It wouldn't surprise me if it was, and bloody good riddance if it turns out to be him. Disgusting pervert of a man, he was. Used to make my skin crawl when he looked at me."

"Where did you work at the factory?" Sally asked.

"On the shopfloor. He had his eye on a few of us. Of course, we didn't know that at the time. The rumours began after he went missing. Personally, I put the flags out and started rejoicing as soon as I heard the news, so did Dean."

"Why did Dean react that way? Did he work at the factory as well?" Sally took a sip from her mug.

"No, but he'd visited the factory a few months before..." Her voice drifted off, and she stared down at her clenched hands.

"May I ask why?"

"To deal with the shitbag."

"Deal with him? In what way?"

"After what Coppell did to me, and no, I'd rather not go into the nitty-gritty of what that pervert put me through. Dean couldn't hold back. He visited the factory one night and beat the fucking crap out of Coppell. I couldn't stop him.

I was there. As soon as Coppell saw me and Dean together, he realised what was about to happen and tried to make a run for it, but Dean pounced on the fucking weasel and wiped the bloody floor with him. There was blood everywhere, and I don't regret saying this, but I didn't feel guilty in the slightest. Bastards like that shouldn't have been allowed to have gone on the prowl like he did. It was up to people like us, or should I say my Dean, to do the decent thing and teach the effing shit a lesson, once and for all."

"Once and for all? Care to elaborate?"

"Not really. Why? Why are you here asking all these questions, over twenty years later? You think this body has something to do with me?"

"I'm not suggesting it has anything to do with you. We've carried out extensive enquiries that have highlighted a possible name for the victim."

"It is him, isn't it?"

"There's a distinct possibility, yes."

"Can I ask how you've come to that conclusion?"

"We've yet to have it confirmed by the pathologist, she's carrying out extensive tests on the remains and should have the results soon, however, the remains were discovered on the site of Coppell's old cottage."

"What? But we were led to believe that he'd taken off, deserted his wife and kids. Not that they were that bothered at being dumped. Bugger, you don't suppose the wife did it, do you?"

"It's a possibility. We're in the process of gathering all the information we can find about Coppell and we've been surprised to learn what a dangerous and volatile man he actually was."

"And some. That's why Dean went down there to sort him out. He couldn't let the fucker get away with treating women like that. Not only did he disrespect his wife and kids but he also treated every woman who crossed his path abysmally and with as much hatred as he could muster. He was a damn monster, and that fucking Simmons allowed him to get away with it."

"You believe Simmons knew?"

"Undoubtedly. You could see it on his face. He lost weight, became gaunt, the second the rumours started flying."

"And you believe what? That he covered up the offences rather than tackle them head-on?"

"Yes, I honestly believe that. Look, I'm telling you, no bloody woman was safe if she was left on her own with Coppell. He pounced on several of the girls, me included. I've always considered myself willing and able to fend for myself, however, he had me beat. But when it came to dealing with men, such as the time Dean showed up at the factory, he tried to frigging run a mile. Fucking gutless coward, he was. Sounds to me like he got his just desserts and the person who killed him deserves a medal. I'd be the first to give it to them, too."

"Can you go over what he did to you?"

"I'd rather not. It was callous and degrading. His strength took me by surprise and knocked me off balance. I tried to stand up to him but I was no match for him, just like he wasn't for my Dean."

"Is Dean usually a violent man?"

"No, before that he'd never been involved in any type of aggro. He was merely sticking up for me. Prepared to fight for my honour. That's what you call a real man, not one who goes around raping women, just for the bloody sake of it."

"I agree. Although, your husband shouldn't have taken things into his own hands. Why didn't you go to the police and report the crime?"

"Because… let's face it, twenty years ago, the police didn't give a flying fuck if women got raped or not. I'm not even sure they do today, either judging by the recent breaking news bulletins about the sodding Met Police. We're supposed to trust you lot and yet…"

Sally held her hands up. "That's a different force entirely. DS Warner here used to work for the Met, and she's told me it was a different culture down there to what we have up here. You should have trusted us to have dealt with the rapist, if that's what he was."

"Believe me, he was. To my knowledge, he raped five or more women at that factory. Every woman was wary of him getting close to her because of his wandering hands. He was known as 'Cop-a-grope Coppell' back in the day. You should have heard the sigh of relief break out when the news got out that he'd taken off."

"What response did you get from Simmons when you filed a complaint with him? You did file one, didn't you?"

"I did, and a lot of good it did me… not. He didn't want to know, told me that I had misinterpreted the signals and that Coppell was only being friendly, ensuring that everyone got on with their roles in a happy environment. I came home that night and told Dean everything."

"Wait, up until then you hadn't told your husband about the rape?"

"No, it's not something that came naturally to me. My husband and I don't tell each other every secret we have. Do you with your husband?"

Sally shrugged. "Sorry, but yes."

"Oh, well, I suppose we all have different ways of dealing with our partners. Most men I know wouldn't give a toss if their wives had a hair appointment or were going out for drinks with their friends. That type of thing."

"It's slightly different to reveal that you had been sexually assaulted."

"Exactly. I couldn't not tell Dean. I've never seen him so angry. When Dean got hold of him, the coward wasn't fighting back. One of the drivers eventually pulled Dean off Coppell. If he hadn't... well, I dread to think what the consequences would have been. We drove off not long after, didn't even bother to check if Coppell was badly injured or not. He was moving when we left him, that was good enough for us."

"And was he okay, the next day at work?"

"He had a couple of shiners, nothing more than he deserved. I caught a passing glimpse of him in the corridor at the end of my shift. He avoided my section that day, which was a relief to everyone."

"And when did this incident take place in relation to Coppell going missing?"

"A week or so before. In between, Coppell was really sheepish. Didn't show his face much, not like he usually did during the working day."

"Did you know his wife and girls?"

"I'd met them a couple of times at work functions, you know the type of thing, Christmas bashes and a picnic in the grounds of the factory in the summer."

"How did they react to being at these events?"

"They all stood in the corner, a plate of uneaten nibbles in their hands while he circulated the crowd like butter wouldn't melt. Such an insincere prick, but most people saw through him."

"All except Greg Simmons, eh?" Lorne said.

"So it would seem. Maybe he regarded Coppell worth his weight in gold as a manager. What do you think?" Sally asked.

Alessia shrugged. "If that's what you believe, I've never really thought about it."

"Did Dean only attack Coppell the once?"

"Yes, although he showed up now and again to keep Coppell in line."

"He did? And what happened when Dean came to the factory?"

"Nothing, he waited outside the gate, glaring at Coppell to make sure he knew he was keeping an eye on him. In my opinion, it did the trick because Coppell never came near me again."

"And did Coppell ever make any threats towards Dean? By that I mean, did he warn him what would occur if Dean ever laid a hand on him in the future?"

"No, which was kind of unexpected. I warned Dean to back off, felt that it wouldn't take much for Coppell to come up with a cock-and-bull story as to why he'd beaten him. I was confused. I spent the next week in turmoil. My mind in a whirl, it was like living under a cloud of oppression. Hard to explain, but the only positive that came out of the bashing Dean dished out was that Coppell kept his distance from all the girls right up until he left or vanished, whichever way you want to look at it."

"What about the men at the factory, were there any apart from Greg Simmons?"

"Yes, there was another manager there, I can't for the life of me remember what his name was, but he dealt with the delivery side of things as opposed to Coppell, whose job it was to oversee the manufacturing arm of the business."

"And the delivery drivers, how many were there?"

"Three, I think. You're really asking me to dig deep now. The main one was Sid Parrish, he was a decent bloke. If he's still around, it might be worth having a word with him if you can. There's something stuck in my memory about him, but I can't quite recall what it was."

"Don't worry, we'll see if we can find him. Thanks so

much for speaking with us today and shedding some light on what it was like working at the factory around that time."

"You're welcome. Sorry I couldn't have been more help, like supplying more names for you to chase up. I guess the memory isn't what it used to be these days."

"Don't worry, you've given us something useful to go on, that's more than we had when we arrived. Take care of yourself."

They left the house, and Sally checked the notes in her notebook.

"Ah, that's interesting. I've got Sid Parrish's name copied down from the complaint file Greg Simmons showed me."

"And yet the name didn't ring a bell with you when it was mentioned? That's not a criticism by the way," Lorne added.

"No. I suppose I only really took notice of the women's names for obvious reasons. Let's pop over there, it's not far from here, and see what he has to say for himself."

"Are there many more to see now?"

"Just Vera Bond, after him. Hopefully, we can squeeze her in afterwards."

"It's pushing it," Lorne replied.

Sally glanced at the clock on the dashboard. It was almost four.

"I don't mind working longer," Lorne said. "The decision is yours, though."

"Thanks, Lorne. We'll see how things go and make the call later. I'd really like to get all the witnesses out of the way tonight, then we can collate everything the team has cobbled together and see where that leads us in the morning."

"Sounds like a plan."

SID PARRISH LIVED in an assisted-living bungalow on the outskirts of Attleborough. He answered the door using a walking frame, his back curved, and he limped when he led them into the lounge. Sally watched him struggle to sit in the high-backed armchair and cringed.

"We appreciate you seeing us at short notice, Mr Parrish," Sally said with a smile.

"It's no bother. I'm intrigued to know what this is all about. How can I help? It's Sid by the way."

"We're dealing with an investigation where human remains were found on a construction site."

He eased forward in his chair. "How interesting. Well, don't stop there. What's that got to do with me? I hope you're not insinuating that I put the bloody body there, are you?" He tipped back his head and laughed.

Once he'd stopped splitting his sides, Sally smiled. "I hope not. However, the discovery has led us to question a few of your former work colleagues at Simmons' Steels."

The smile on his face vanished, and a thunderous expression replaced it. "That place? Why? Who have you spoken to?"

Sally revealed the list of names of the witnesses they'd spoken to so far. All the time, he sat there tutting and shaking his head, his cheeks growing redder and redder.

"That place turned out to be the bane of my life. I should never have got involved in all that crap. I was a driver and should have left it at that and simply got on with my job."

"Why didn't you? I'm guessing it's because you're a decent chap who couldn't abide watching your female colleagues being taken advantage of."

"That was part of it. The flipside of that was I hate seeing men abusing their positions, and boy, did that pervert do that."

"Are you talking about Paul Coppell?" Sally asked.

"Aren't you?" he responded, perplexed. "Is there another reason you're here? He was a bloody sex pest. Had the women over a barrel only because of the position he was in with the company. Despicable human being, and I told him so on more than one occasion."

"Care to tell us about that?"

"I caught him red-handed in the warehouse. He thought all the drivers were out. I should have been, I'd nipped to the loo. I was walking through the warehouse on the way to my lorry when I heard what sounded like a woman crying out for help. Well, I went towards the noise, thought I'd find someone with a box on top of them having tripped over or something. I couldn't have been more wrong. What I found absolutely disgusted me." He shook his head and shuddered. "Even today, it appals me to think what those women must have gone through. I'd heard rumours but I was never one for listening to gossip, I'd rather make up my own mind about someone, and I certainly did on that day."

"What did you see, Sid?"

"I saw Paul Coppell with his hands up Vera Bond's skirt. Now this surprised me in two ways, first seeing a bloody manager getting himself in that position, and second, Vera, she wasn't the type to put up with that shit. She was a mouthy individual who usually stuck up for herself. I suppose you don't really know how someone is going to react when they're overpowered like that."

"And how did they both react when you stepped closer, caught them, or should I say Coppell, in the act?"

"He was mortified. Backed away pretty smart, brushed himself down and accused Vera of leading him on. By this time, poor Vera was distraught and in tears, sobbing, she was. I asked her if he'd forced himself upon her. She nodded, and that was enough for me. I knocked him to the floor with a right and then a left hook, effing moron. He was gross. He shouldn't have been allowed to get away with what he did.

Greg Simmons didn't frigging want to know. I had my cards marked the day I put in the complaint."

"You spoke up for Vera? That was kind of you."

"Kindness didn't come into it, love—sorry, Inspector. I know what's right and wrong, and he was a fucking wrong 'un, there was no mistaking that."

"And Vera put in a complaint at the same time, did she?"

"That's right. I had to persuade her to do it. Apparently, he'd assaulted her a couple of times before that, and she'd never plucked up the courage to speak out against him because he was a damn manager and she was desperate to keep hold of her job. Well, screw that. Women have rights as well as men. She and the other girls had a right to carry out their jobs without someone touching them up inappropriately."

"I agree with you. You're to be admired for speaking up for the women."

"To be admired, that's a joke. They sacked me within a week of making the damn complaint. Made up a shit story about me driving erratically and that there had been complaints from customers I'd delivered to who weren't keen on my attitude when I dropped the goods off. Absolute bullshit, it was." He waved a hand. "It's all in the past, I've moved on since then, we all have. There are not many of the older ones left at that factory now, and that bastard did a runner, at least that's what I heard. Walked out on his wife and kids not long after. Maybe his conscience pricked him in the end, who bloody knows? I haven't got a clue what goes on in the mind of a depraved animal like that. I wish to God I had put him in hospital that day. Maybe then he would have thought twice about touching up the girls. His sort never learn, do they? Once a sex pest, always one. Gross! I felt sorry for his wife and kids. I'd heard that she was relieved when he took off. I think I would have been putting the flags out and dancing down the bloody high street if that was me."

Sally laughed. She liked this man, he was refreshingly honest and open with his views. "I think I would have been the same."

He frowned and settled back in his seat. "So, go on, tell me why you're really here. What does all of this have to do with the body you found? You didn't say where the construction site was either. Care to tell me?"

"Okay, the site was over in Watton. The row of cottages where Coppell used to live."

He inched forward again and winced. "Damn hip, sometimes I forget how much gyp it gives me. I'm due to have an operation at the end of the month, I can't bloody wait. Sod what pain I'm in afterwards, it can't be any worse than what I've been dealing with the last couple of years."

"It must be hard living in constant pain every day."

"It is, there's no doubt about it. Hang on, going over what you just told me, who do you think the body belongs to? Did he eventually go on to kill someone?"

Sally shrugged. "We're still awaiting the confirmation from the post-mortem, however, there's every indication that the remains might belong to Coppell himself."

"What the actual fuck, are you kidding me? But he ran off... bugger, or did he? Was that something the family put around? Did they bump him off? That wife of his finally had enough of his shitty behaviour and bashed him over the head with a shovel, did she?" He laughed. "Sorry, I shouldn't make light of it, someone losing their life is a very serious matter, except we're talking about Coppell here. A frigging menace and a half to society who needed bumping off, in my opinion. Well, I never! What a shocking revelation that was."

"It's a line of enquiry open to us. Of course, there's every chance we might be barking up the wrong tree, suspecting the remains belong to Coppell."

"But it would be nice to think someone got the better of him and rid this world of the bastard after what he put his family and his co-workers through, right?"

"Possibly."

"Goodness me, I wish I'd been there. You know, if someone did kill him, I would have loved to have seen him suffer before he snuffed it. Am I wrong to think that? I don't think I am, he was such a vile person. He deserved everything he got in the end."

"If it's him," Sally added with caution.

"Who else could it possibly be if it was found on his property?"

Sally shrugged. "That's just it, we believe the remains were found next door. We've yet to track down the owners of number six to see what their side of the story is."

He laughed again. "Bloody hell, the plot thickens. So someone did away with him and buried him next door. Sounds like a bloody Sherlock Holmes novel, doesn't it? *The Body Buried Next Door.*" Again, he laughed.

Sally had trouble suppressing the chuckle desperate to break free. "Anyway, until we do find the property owners, we're doing our very best to form a picture of what Coppell was like at home and at work."

"Forgive me for saying this, but if you haven't formed a picture by now, you're never going to. You said you've spoken to all the women he touched up, and did they reveal the truth?"

"Yes, none of them have held back. We've only got Vera Bond to interview now, she'll be our final call for the day."

"I'm sure she'll corroborate what I've told you. There's no reason for her not to. Bloody hell, I can't get over knowing that he might be dead, after all these years of people thinking he'd moved on to pastures new. I must say, the first thing I thought about when I'd heard he'd taken off was I pity the poor women he encounters along the way. No woman deserves to be treated the way he treated the girls working at that factory, or his wife and kids. I'm glad someone killed him, rid this world of a pathetic sex pest like that. What a shock this has all been. A bloody shock, I tell you."

"Sorry, we didn't mean to cause you any upset by coming here today."

"Oh, no, you haven't. It's still a shock, though."

"Is there anything else you can tell us about your time working at the factory that you believe we should be looking at during this investigation?"

"By that, do you mean was there anything dodgy going on?"

"Yes. Or anyone else we should interview?"

"Have you questioned the main man, Greg Simmons? He brushed a hell of a lot under the carpet at the time. Not interested in anything damning that went on in his treasured factory and anyone who dared to speak out against the bad things happening was dealt with."

"By being sacked?" Sally asked.

"That's right. Shameful behaviour. These bosses have got to realise the workers have rights. From a female point of view, no one should need to go to work on their guard just in case anything untoward happens to them during the course of the day. Isn't that classed as an unsafe working environment these days?"

"The laws have changed since twenty years ago, I agree. Coppell should never have been allowed to get away with his behaviour. Okay, then we're going to leave you to it and shoot over to see if we can catch Vera in. We can't thank you enough for being open and honest with us today."

"You're welcome. I hope you solve the mystery as to who killed the fucker, if it turns out to be that mongrel."

"I'm sure we will. Thanks again. Here's my card if you remember anything else you think we should know in the future."

"I'll pop it on the sideboard so I don't lose it."

Sally held her hand up. "Stay there, we'll see ourselves out and close the door behind us, save you getting up."

"I won't argue with you."

CHAPTER 8

*T*heir final stop of the day was postponed for ten minutes while Sally spoke to the pathologist who rang her mobile en route to Vera Bond's house. Sally pulled into a nearby car park and put the phone on speaker. "Hi, Pauline. What have you got for me? I hope it's a positive ID."

"It is. Thanks to the DNA samples we received from Erica and Paige, we've formally identified the victim as their father, Paul Coppell."

"Wow, that's fabulous, however, the news wasn't unexpected, was it? Am I pushing my luck asking what the likely cause of death was?"

"At this stage, yes. Although I can disclose that we discovered a fracture in the base of the skull. My best guesstimate is that he suffered a blow to the head which most likely killed him."

"Blunt force trauma, is that what you're saying?"

"Exactly, but it's not official, not yet. How's your investigation going?"

"Let's put it this way, I don't think anyone will be crying once the news gets out. The man was an utterly despicable human being, not that I would wish anyone dead, but I sense it was only a matter of time before someone bumped him off. Let's just say the suspect list is growing, and fast."

"Oh, I see. I'm not sure what to make of that statement. Care to enlighten me with some of the details you've uncovered?"

"He was a sex pest of the highest order. Not only that, he abused his position as a manager and, furthermore, the owner of the factory where all this took place was willing to turn a blind eye to the complaints when they started rolling in."

"Jesus fucking Christ, what's wrong with people? There are laws about harassment at work."

"Yeah, something that seems to have been disregarded or overlooked at this establishment. Maybe it's different these days, after all we're talking twenty-odd years ago."

"Possibly. Right, I must get on. I'll pass on your thanks to the lab for pushing the results through for you."

Sally punched her thigh. "Sorry, I'm slapping my wrist. I should have said that, it's not like me to be so ignorant, I promise."

"End of the day, and you've had a pig of one by the sounds of it, so I'll let you off this time. Have a good evening, Sally."

"I will. Thanks again to you and your team for an outstanding effort."

"There's no need to go over the top." Pauline ended the call.

Sally breathed out a heavy sigh. "So we were right all along, it is him."

"Too much of a coincidence not to be. All we need to do now is find the murderer."

Sally faced her partner and rolled her eyes. "Yeah, easy, right?"

"As you've mentioned already, the suspect list is growing.

What we have to consider is whether any of the victims would have it in them to kill him."

"One person is sticking out in my mind." Sally raised an eyebrow, expecting Lorne to fill in the blank.

"Dean Kane?"

Sally nodded. "It might be worth having a chat with him, but we can do that tomorrow. Let's see what Vera Bond has to say for herself first. Do me a favour, ring the team, see if they can find out who this other manager is. I think we could do with speaking to him."

"I'll get on to them now."

VERA LIVED in an old cottage on the outskirts of Ashill which was within a stone's throw of Watton. She was tending to her garden when they arrived.

"Hello, is it Mrs Bond?"

"It's Miss. And you are?" She pulled herself to her feet, aided by her walking stick.

"Can you manage?"

"Of course. I'm a little doddery on my pins. Bending down affects the circulation in case you don't know."

Sally considered herself told and apologised. She produced her warrant card. "We're DI Sally Parker and DS Lorne Warner. Would it be convenient to have a chat with you in private?"

"Are you going to tell me what this is about?"

"Your time working at Simmons' Steels."

Anger seemed to hit Vera at full pelt. "Are you kidding me?" she shouted. "What the hell? That was over twenty years ago, and here you are, standing in my garden wanting to discuss it. Why?"

"It really would be better if we spoke inside."

"I'm busy, surely you can see that."

Sally got the impression the woman was bubbling with anger inside. "I wouldn't ask if it wasn't vital to the investigation we're working on."

"What investigation? What has that company been up to now? As if I didn't know the answer to that already."

Vera seemed a little calmer, in Sally's opinion.

"It would be better if we spoke inside, away from any possible flapping ears and prying eyes."

"Hey, stop insulting my neighbours, that's my job, and you're spot on with your analysis, they are nosey beggars."

Sally's smile matched Vera's, and the older woman led the way around the side of the house to the back door. The rear garden was in better nick than the front, if that was at all possible.

"Your gardens are lovely. Do you spend a lot of time out here?"

"Yes. I had to take early retirement due to ill health. Don't ask, bone cancer. I'm living day to day, hoping that a miracle cure can be found soon. Can't see it happening in my lifetime, but you never know. My garden has been my saviour, giving life to these plants. Watching them flourish truly brightens my day. I can spend hours out here and not even realise it."

"Sounds a wonderful escape. I'm sorry your health isn't better. The gardens are a credit to you and all the hard work you've put in."

"Thank you. Come in. You needn't take your shoes off, the kitchen floor is tiled. Can I get you ladies a drink?"

"No, thank you. You're our last stop for the day, and then we'll be going home."

"Must be nice being an officer on the day shift with the lighter evenings for you to enjoy when you get home."

"It's definitely a bonus."

She invited them to sit at the round pine kitchen table

that looked out of place against the modern darker units and granite worktops. "Okay, now that I've calmed down, you can tell me why you're making enquiries about that horrible place, which I never thought I'd hear mentioned again in my lifetime, however long that is likely to be now."

Sally sat opposite the woman and smiled awkwardly. She retold the story of discovering the body at the construction site for the umpteenth time in the past forty-eight hours or more and what they had learned from the other witnesses in that time, regarding the disgusting behaviour Coppell was allowed to get away with at the factory. "Actually, before I let you speak, there's one more snippet of information you should know that might help with your decision as to whether or not you want to speak with us about your experience back in the day."

"And that is?"

"On the way here, we received a call from the pathologist. She's confirmed the remains belong to Paul Coppell."

Vera let out the breath she'd sucked in moments earlier and reclined in her seat, allowing the rigidness to seep out of her shoulders and back. "Thank God for that. I'm sorry if that makes me come across as a heartless bitch, but what an absolute relief that news is going to be to the women he's ever laid a hand on. I can't be the only one who has lived under a storm cloud all these years."

Sally nodded. "I have to hold my hand up and admit that I totally agree with you. By what the others have told us, including his wife and daughters, if anyone deserved to die it was him." She leaned in and whispered, "Of course I will deny ever saying that. As a police officer it is my job to always be impartial. Sometimes that's far easier than others. From what my partner and I have been told by the victims who worked at the factory, and again his own family, then I think he's earned the right to be the exception to the rule."

"Well said, boss," Lorne agreed.

She smiled and gave Lorne a brief nod of acceptance.

Vera heaved out a sigh and said, "The thing is, it could have, and should have, all been avoided, if only Simmons had listened to us all. I agree, if one tale had come out, the likelihood of it being true would have been debatable, but you've seen for yourself how many women stepped forward and accused that bastard... for what? To be treated as if they themselves were the criminals, rather than the actual rapist."

"That must have been absolutely devastating for all concerned."

"It was immoral and should never have been allowed to have happened, ever."

"Speaking with a few of the victims, a couple of them mentioned another manager being on site that maybe could have helped but didn't. I wondered if you might be able to recall his name. You see, the others couldn't, and we'd love to question him as part of our investigation."

"Good call. He should be grilled. I'd love to hear what his excuse was for not speaking out at the time. That bloody Simmons couldn't have given a toss, I can tell you. Let me think now, it's been a while, as you're aware." She stared out of the back window at the pretty pink double roses in bloom, her eyes forming tiny slits as she thought. Then, out of the blue, she clicked her fingers and said, "I know, it's just come to me. His surname jumped into my mind and then his first name followed shortly after."

Sally inched forward in her seat. "And it is?"

"Sorry, yes, it's Roland Evans."

Sally's neck clicked as she faced Lorne swiftly, both of them shocked by the news.

"Have I said something wrong? Are you going to tell me what's going on here?" Vera asked, her voice becoming taut again, just like it had been when they'd first arrived on her doorstep.

"We've been trying to trace him but had no luck. As far as we know he lives in Norwich somewhere. This is the first we've heard about him working at the factory, let alone being a manager. Do you know if he's still there?"

"As far as I know but you'll have to check how accurate that is for yourself."

Lorne's phone rang. "I'll take this in the back garden. Excuse me, won't you?"

"Of course. Go right ahead," Vera said.

Sally couldn't help but be distracted by her partner's absence and was eager to hear the news when Lorne rejoined them a few minutes later. "Well, anything I should know?"

"It's been confirmed by the team, Roland Evans still works there."

Sally scraped back her chair and apologised to Vera. "I'm sorry, we're going to have to leave now, we need to have a word with Evans before the day is out. Can we call back and see you another time?" Sally slid one of her business cards across the table.

"Go, yes, I'm not clocking out on life for a while yet, so feel free to come back another time, I'm always here. Good luck. Will you tell me what the significance is before you leave?"

"Evans was Coppell's neighbour. It was their row of cottages that formed the construction site where Coppell's remains were found buried in concrete. We believe that occurred at number six, Evans' house."

Vera gasped. "My God, you think he killed him?"

"It's beginning to look that way. We have to shoot over there, see if we can catch him before he leaves work for the day."

Vera glanced up at the large kitchen clock over to her

right. "You should make it in time. What an eye-opener, eh? I never thought I'd live to see the day I heard such news about someone I knew."

"Thanks for all your assistance, you've probably helped us solve the mystery to this case."

"Unknowingly, eh?"

"They all count. Thanks again. Sorry to run out on you like this, we'll catch up with you soon."

Sally and Lorne darted out of the back door and ran around the side of the house to the car. Inside, they strapped themselves in.

Sally turned the key in the ignition and said, "Call the station back and tell Jordan and Stuart to head over to the factory. Tell them to wait outside until we arrive. We should get there around the same time, by the skin of our teeth and with fifteen minutes to spare."

CHAPTER 9

*S*ally's pulse raced the closer they got to the factory gates. Stuart and Jordan parked alongside them in the road adjacent to the large building. Sally wanted there to be an element of surprise when they showed up.

"Are you ready for this?" she asked the three members of her team.

"More than ready, I'd say," Lorne chipped in.

"Okay, let's see what Mr Evans has to say for himself."

They walked through the reception area which was empty.

A door opened at the end of the corridor, and the receptionist appeared. "I'm so sorry to have kept you waiting, I was sourcing a file I needed from the cabinet. How can I help?"

"We'd like to see Roland Evans. Is he still here?"

"Ah, yes. I've just seen him in the storage area. I'll text him, ask him to come and see you."

"Thanks, that would be really helpful."

She did the necessary with her mobile and returned to her station. The same door opened at the end of the hallway, and a man in his late fifties, dressed in a grey pinstriped suit, came towards them.

"You wanted to speak with me?" Evans asked Sally.

"I did. You're an elusive man, Mr Evans, we've been trying to track you down for a few days."

"Sorry, had I known I would have contacted you. I've been away on a course. What can I do for you?"

Sally showed her ID. "I'm DI Sally Parker, and these are members of my Cold Case team."

"All right, should that mean something to me?"

"We'd like you to accompany us to the station for further questioning, sir."

"Questioning? May I ask what it's in connection with?"

"You may. The body found buried under the extension of your former property in Watton."

The colour in his face drained, and his legs wobbled.

Sally thought he was going to pass out. "Are you all right?"

"I... umm... I think so."

"Do you have anything to say in response?"

"No, not really. Should I call my solicitor?"

"If you have one that deals with criminal law, by all means get in touch with them. You can do it from the car."

"What's going on here?" Greg Simmons bellowed from the other end of the long passageway.

"It's all right, Greg. I'm going to the station to help the police with their enquiries, it's nothing to worry about."

"What? Can't you interview him here, like you did with me?"

"No, we'd prefer to have the interview recorded back at the station, sir. There's no need for you to be concerned."

"Bullshit! You come here mob-handed and tell me it's nothing to worry about. I demand to know why it takes four of you to turn up and collect one of my managers."

"Mr Evans is an intrinsic part of our investigation," Sally retorted. She could tell Simmons was trying to contain his anger, and failing, judging by the colour rising up his neck and flooding into his cheeks.

"I see. Do you need me to call the company lawyer, Roland?"

"No, I've got my own, thanks, Greg."

"Let me know later how you got on."

Jordan and Stuart stood either side of Evans, and Sally led the way with Lorne back to the cars.

Outside the vehicle, Sally advised, "You'd better call your solicitor before he goes home for the evening."

Roland slipped his hand into his jacket pocket and removed his phone. "What shall I tell him?"

Sally grinned. "What you told Simmons, that you're helping us with our enquiries."

The four team members shuffled their feet until Evans had placed his call.

"He's going to go straight to the station."

"Good, let's get to it," Sally replied.

Stuart placed Evans in the back of his car, and they returned to the station in a mini convoy.

"How are you going to play this?" Lorne asked en route.

"I'm not going to dilly-dally, I'm just going to come right out and ask him. Why? How would you play it?"

Lorne grinned. "The same. We've spent most of the week gathering evidence. What we need now is the cold hard facts to draw the investigation to a swift conclusion."

"I agree with you one hundred percent."

THE DESK SERGEANT had set up Interview Room One ready for their arrival. Sally thanked Stuart and Jordan for the part they'd played and asked them to wait upstairs.

Inside the room, with his solicitor, Mr Peterson, Evans looked nervous as the interview commenced.

"I wish to thank you first of all, Mr Evans, for agreeing to attend this interview of your own free will."

"I didn't think I really had an option," he mumbled in response.

His solicitor leaned over and whispered something in his ear. Sally groaned inside, suspecting what Evans had just been instructed to do.

"As you're probably aware, we've been at Simmons' Steels this week, interviewing the owner and chasing up former members of staff who raised grievances with the company."

"I wasn't aware. As I told you before, I've been away on a course the past few days."

"May I ask where?"

"In Liverpool. It was a delivery update course. What to expect now that we've come out of Europe. Some firms are struggling to deal with the new procedures that have been put in place after Brexit."

"Thank you for the insight. So, am I to believe that you haven't been told anything about what's occurred in your absence?"

"That's correct. What has been going on? I heard rumours that you've been questioning the former staff of the factory."

"We have. What we'd really like to know is how the remains of your former colleague, Paul Coppell, were buried in concrete at your property."

"I don't know," he replied quickly, without hesitation.

His solicitor whispered something else in his ear.

"Why are you being so cagey about this, Mr Evans? It seems pretty obvious to me that you killed your colleague and buried him before the extension to your property was erected."

"No comment," he said. His head dipped, and his gaze focused on his linked hands.

And here it is, going down the bloody 'no comment' route, as usual. Give me a break! "Hard to deny you had nothing to do with his murder when the finger of doubt is pointing in your direction, Mr Evans. Why don't you save us all a lot of time and admit you killed him?"

"No comment."

The questions kept coming, but Sally received the same response until she switched tack and brought Coppell's wife and daughters into the conversation. "Why do you suppose he was killed? Because of Tina, Paige and Erica? Because of the pain and torment they went through? Did you hear it through the walls? Was it hard to listen to?"

"No comment."

Sally sensed he was approaching breaking point, judging by the intensity of his hand movements. "Did the girls' screams get to you? I should imagine anyone would go ballistic and smash him on the back of the head. I wonder if it was their intention to kill him. Or was it their aim to fire a warning shot in the hope he would back off and leave the girls alone? No one likes to hear defenceless kids pleading with their own father to stop beating them, do they? You'd have to be a cold-hearted type of person not to let that affect you, wouldn't you? Maybe that's what happened, the day he was killed."

Silence. He didn't issue a "no comment" response this time, so Sally pushed on.

"Did you ever lie there at night, with your teeth gritted, wishing that you had the guts to go around there and have it out with him?"

"Every fucking night. The same routine over and over. I had to do something to help those girls."

"Roland, I must advise you not to say anything further," Peterson said.

"I can't stand it any more. I've lived with the guilt of knowing that I was a part of his murder for years and I can't take the secret to my grave. I thought I could, but I can't."

Lorne and Sally nudged each other's legs under the table.

"Part of his murder?" Sally queried. "I don't understand. You're going to need to divulge more, Mr Evans, Roland. Come on, I can tell you want to relieve yourself of the guilt. Let it out, free yourself once and for all."

He gulped and shook his head. "I can't," he whispered.

"I'm sorry, you're going to have to speak up for the recording, Mr Evans. What did you say?"

"I can't. We made a pact. I refuse to be the one to break it."

"A pact, with Tina?"

He shook his head again and groaned. "No, she was in the dark about all of this. That poor woman suffered at the hands of that pervert for too many years. How she had the courage to overcome the beatings he gave her and carry on, I'll never know. But I can tell you she played no part in his murder at all."

"Then who? His daughters?"

His head tipped back, he closed his eyes and released a shuddering breath. "Just the one."

"The older one, Paige?"

He nodded.

"Did Coppell rape her?"

"Yes, frequently, but it wasn't because of that. I've said too much, it's up to her to fill in the rest of the details for you. She sent out a cry for help, and I did what I could to assist her, however, just because his body was buried in my foundations, it doesn't mean that I killed him. I'm not going down for his actual murder."

"You're telling me that Paige killed her own father, is that right?"

He nodded.

"For the recording, you nodded, is that correct?"

"Yes."

Sally ended the interview there and then. She exited the room and went in search of the custody sergeant to request Evans be arrested for aiding and abetting a murderer. Then, she and Lorne left the station and drove out to Tina's address.

"ARE you going to get her to ask the girls over?" Lorne asked en route.

"We're almost there now. Yes, let's see what Tina's reaction is first and go from there."

"I'm with you all the way. What a bloody revelation this is. Paige must have been desperate to have killed him, teetering on the brink for years if he'd abused their mother and then turned his attention upon her. You can't imagine what she must have gone through, can you?"

"It doesn't bear thinking about, however, that doesn't excuse Paige for killing her father. I still have questions I want to ask Evans, but they can wait, this can't. If word gets out that we have him in custody, there's a possibility Paige might do a runner."

"You believe his wife is in on it, too, and that she might warn her daughter?"

"I'm just covering all the bases right now, Lorne. I think you would have done the same if you were in my shoes."

"I would. Want me to call home, tell them we'll be late?"

"Ring Tony, he can pass on the message to Simon."

"He's not going to like that, hearing it second-hand. Have you rung him during the day to patch things up?"

"Bugger off, when have I had the time to do that? You've been with me every second of the damn day."

"All right, I was only teasing you."

Lorne rang Tony who was a little disappointed to hear they were going to be late until she gave him the lowdown on what was going on and how important it was for them to follow through that night. He agreed and promised to give Simon a call as soon as she hung up.

"Done and dusted. Two pissed-off husbands for us to contend with when we eventually get home."

Sally groaned. "I might put my head down in the office tonight instead."

Lorne laughed. "That's carrying things to the extreme, boss."

"I know, but what's the alternative? Right, we're here, game faces on, ready for action."

"Okay, you've got it. Why didn't you feel the need to bring backup with us?"

"Christ, if we can't handle a group of women between us, one with cancer, then we really are in the wrong job, Lorne."

"Go on then, you've twisted my arm. I'm up for it if you are."

"Too right." Sally drew up outside Tina's house and spotted the sick woman looking out of her lounge window. "We've been clocked. She seems relaxed enough to see us."

"If Evans is to be believed, Tina had nothing to do with the murder. How are we going to get Paige or both the girls to come over without raising their suspicions?"

"Leave it to me."

They exited the car. Sally waved at Tina, who smiled and waved back then left her viewing point. Within seconds the front door opened, and she welcomed them into her home once more.

"It's nice to see you both again. Does this mean you have news for me?"

"For all of you. Is it possible for you to give your daughters a ring, ask them to join us before I share the news?" Sally smiled. "I swear, it'll be worth their while coming over."

"Oh, that does sound intriguing. Let me give them a call right away. Won't you ladies take a seat in the lounge with me?"

"We'd love to." Sally's insides twisted themselves into a huge knot, and she snuck a glance at Lorne who winked at her.

Tina made the two calls, and they waited for her daughters to arrive. Erica was the first to join them ten minutes later, and a sheepish-looking Paige entered the lounge a couple of minutes after that.

Now it was up to Sally to pin the tail on the donkey, so to speak. "Thank you for joining us this evening, Erica and Paige."

"Why have we been summoned?" Paige was the first to ask.

"Please, take a seat, ladies. I promised I would bring you up to date with any developments we made, so that's what I intend to do."

Sally noticed the look of concern which travelled between the two daughters as they sat on either side of their mum's armchair. *Was it just Paige involved or both of them?*

"Okay, we're listening," Paige said, obviously taking up the role of spokesperson for the family.

"It has been confirmed that the body found at the construction site is that of your father, Paul Coppell."

"What?" Tina shouted, disbelief etched into her features.

Her daughters gripped each of her hands.

"All right Mum, don't overreact, let's see what the inspector has to say," Paige said.

"Thank you, Paige. Sorry, Tina, I know this must have come as a shock to you, however, there are certain people in this room who were already aware your husband was dead. Isn't that right, Paige and Erica?" Sally said, taking a punt her instinct was correct.

Tina's gaze flitted between her two daughters. She seemed confused and bewildered.

Paige gulped and gripped her mother's hand tighter. "Don't do this, not in front of Mum, have a heart, Inspector. She's not well."

Sally wagged her finger. "Don't do that, Paige, turn the tables on us, making out we're the ones in the wrong, not when, for twenty-plus years, you've kept your nauseating secret from your mother."

Paige mimicked Sally and wagged her finger in return. "Don't make me out to be the bad guy here. You have no idea what that man was capable of. He had to be stopped before he killed one of us. You can't imagine the fear we all woke up with, day after day, not knowing how the abuse would manifest itself during the day ahead. Don't you dare come here and criticise me for dealing with a dangerous situation before it got out of control."

Tina withdrew her hand from both of her daughters' and shook her head. "All this time you've let me believe that he had run off. I had to wait nearly ten years before I could marry the man of my dreams, we wasted all that time because you had dealt with the situation already and couldn't be bothered to tell me. You've made a fool out of me all these years... get out of my sight, Paige."

Paige stared long and hard at her mother, and then her gaze drifted to her sister. Erica had her head down and sobbed.

"I did it for all of us but most of all for Erica. I had lived through the abuse way into my teens, I was determined she wouldn't have to contend with that. Tell them, Erica. I did this for you."

"I didn't want you to. You took it upon yourself that night to get rid of him. I loved him. I know he could be a monster at times, but he was still my father."

Paige's mouth gaped open until she found her voice to offer a rebuttal. "How could you? I'll tell you how… because he hadn't actually raped you *yet*, but it was only a matter of time. I witnessed the hunger he had for you in his eyes. It was killing me. He had to be stopped, and I knew I had to be the one to do it before he killed either you or Mum."

"You should have come to the police for help, Paige. You should never have taken the law into your own hands," Sally said, mixed emotions hurtling through her.

"The police would have come down on his side. He would have managed to talk them around, as usual. More and more stories were emerging from the factory. I knew if I didn't get rid of him things would have only got far worse. Admit it, Mum, the abuse was getting worse, harder and harder every day for you to deal with, wasn't it?"

"It was. But it wasn't up to you to sort things out, that was my responsibility, Paige. You were only seventeen at the time. How, how did you overpower him and kill him?"

"He came home in a foul mood as usual. I later heard that he had been reprimanded at work for showing his true colours. Let's face it, Mum, he was a rapist, pure evil, a sinner through and through, call him what you like, it all amounts to the same thing."

"Will you tell us what happened that night, Paige?" Sally prompted gently.

"Please, Roland wasn't really part of this, all he was trying to do was lend a hand. He was aware of the risks, just like Ian and I were."

"Ian?" Sally asked. "Someone else was involved in the murder?"

Paige's gaze met Sally's. "My husband. He was my fiancé back in the day. I had belted Dad on the head—I don't even want to call him that. A father needs to earn their right to that title, he never did. Tormentor or abuser would be more accurate."

"On that we agree," Tina whispered.

"Mum was out that night, I can't remember where, but I came in from work and saw the look he was giving Erica. I'd seen it myself when I was her age. I knew that he was about to turn his abusive attention on her, soon enough. I was determined not to allow that to happen." Her gaze drifted across the room to a large ebony figure of a woman and a man hugging. "He was his usual vile self that night. I waited until he turned away from me and bashed him round the back of the head. I meant it as a warning of what would happen if he came after either me or Erica again. Ian came in and found me crouched over him. Erica was crying in the corner of the room. He wasn't breathing. I tried to do CPR on him. It went against the grain to try to revive him, but I did my best. However, it was too late."

"Okay, so you were protecting your sister, is that correct?" Sally said, seeing the situation for what it was, self-protection and the protection of a minor from a serial abuser. Aware of Coppell's reputation, she already had it in her mind to speak up for the family when the case went before the CPS. "How did the body get buried next door?"

Paige inhaled a large breath and picked at the skin around her fingernails. "Ian worked for the builder who was laying the foundations at Roland's house. Roland popped by when he heard Erica screaming. He was dumbstruck but shrugged. Told us what had been going on at the factory and said it was bound to happen sooner or later. He came up with the idea of burying him in the foundations which were due to be laid the following day. I don't know the nitty-gritty of that, I left it all to Ian. He told me his boss wasn't going to be around the next day and had put him in charge of overseeing the concrete delivery along with his best friend, Niall. He told me not to worry and that he would dispose of the body. Roland told us to dump Dad's body in his garden, behind the shed until the following day. He was going to set off early on holiday at around nine, so Rita wouldn't know what was going on."

"And when your mother got home, you told her your father had up and left?" Sally completed the story.

"Yes. I'm sorry, I never meant to kill him, it all got out of hand. All I was trying to do was protect my sister." Paige glanced over at Erica who was shaking her head.

"I've lived with the memory of you hitting him with that thing all these years." Erica pointed at the ebony statue on the other side of the room. "He was still my father, you had no right to take that away from me. That thing has been a constant reminder of your evil act."

"I thought I was doing it for the best, for all our sakes, Erica. If I hadn't, Mum wouldn't be with Chris today, she wouldn't have ever experienced what true love was. Yes, she's dealing with cancer but she's surrounded by people who care and love her. You truly think she would have survived this long had she remained married to him?" Paige replied, her voice breaking on the emotion as she fought her corner.

"That should have been my decision to make, Paige, not yours," Tina said. "How could you? How could you sit there, both of you, living a lie, telling me that he had walked out and left me that night?"

"It was my idea, Mum, blame me not Erica. I'm sorry I misjudged the situation. I should have told you the truth, but then you would have been forced to live a life of deceit, and I doubt if you would have ever gone near Chris, would you?"

"No, you're probably right, but we'll never know, will we? Because you saw to that, Paige. You had always hated your father, we could see the defiance in your eyes every day you could bring yourself to look at him. He said he was determined to beat that defiance out of you."

"*And you let him?*" Paige countered, mortified by her mother's admission.

"Don't put words into my mouth. Marriage can be a complex constitution at times. We all have to make compromises at some stage, as you well know with Ian. Your marriage isn't the best, is it? You should have split up long ago, I often wondered why you hadn't, but it's all coming out now... this disgusting secret of yours has ruined all of our lives, without you realising it, hasn't it?"

Paige lowered her head and nodded. "I thought I was doing the right thing, for all of us. It wasn't my intention to kill him, all I wanted to do was warn him to back off."

"But things got out of hand?" Sally chipped in. "I'm sorry, Paige, you know what's going to happen now."

Paige held out her arms. "I do. Arrest me, finally rid me of this guilt."

"I doubt if that will happen overnight, Paige. Tina, Erica, even as an outsider, I can understand that Paige was filled with good intentions. She considers herself as the chief protector of her family, don't fall out about this. I'm not really one for making promises in such circumstances, but you have my word that I will do my very best for you. From what you have told me, your father was killed by a genuine mistake. Years of abuse and your desire to protect your sister culminated in an act of violence that wasn't premeditated. Therefore, we can't throw a murder charge at you, you'll be charged with manslaughter. Tina and Erica, as much as you are hurting inside, I'm going to ask you to try and recall what it was really like living under the same roof as Paul Coppell. Over the coming months, Paige is going to need your support, and especially when the case comes to trial. My advice would be not to throw her under the bus when you get on the stand. She thought she was doing what was right for all of you. Try to remember that on the day."

Paige's crying soon developed into sobs. "I'm sorry," she whispered over and over.

Sally and Lorne rose from their seats. Sally could tell her partner was as emotionally wrought as she was. They led Paige out to the car and placed her in the back seat.

Lorne patted Sally's forearm. "I wholeheartedly agree with what you said back there, Sal. I know I would have handled it in exactly the same way. I take my hat off to you."

"That's all well and good, now all I have to do is convince the CPS. Easy, right?"

EPILOGUE

*T*he day had been spent preparing for that evening's barbecue. Their guests were due to arrive any moment now, and Sally was upstairs with Simon, getting ready for the main event. She threw on her best blouse and glanced out of the window at the orchard. "Lorne and Tony are here."

"I'll be ready in a second," Simon called from the en suite. He came into the bedroom, beaming, and held his arms out, inviting her to walk into them. "Beautiful, you're amazing."

"Get out of here. I slapped a bit of makeup on for a change." She kissed him and then touched up her lipstick again.

The bell rang, and at the same time Lorne called out that they had arrived through the back door.

"Gosh, they've all turned up at once." Sally ran down the stairs and opened the front door to find Jack and Donna standing there.

Her former partner was wearing jeans and a T-shirt, holding a six-pack of beers and a couple of bottles of wine.

"Come in. Welcome to you both."

"Umm... I brought wine, it was Donna's suggestion. I said it was a dumb idea, you know, what with the amount of wine stored in your old man's cellar."

"Every bottle is a pleasure to receive in this house. Lorne has just arrived. Come through to the kitchen, let's get this party started."

"I'm up for that," Simon said from the top of the stairs. "I'll fire up the barbecue and get the food underway. Nice to see you both." He reached the bottom of the stairs and shook Jack's hand. "How are you?"

"Getting there, thanks, Simon."

They drank and ate until the early hours of the morning. Jack had pumped Sally and Lorne for information about the case they had just solved.

"Wow, I bet you didn't see that one coming, eh, Sal?"

"Truthfully, I was leaning towards either the wife being the murderer or Dean Kane. Just goes to show how wrong you can be sometimes. Enough about work, have you decided what hobbies you're going to take up now you're a man of leisure?"

Jack's gaze drifted to his wife and back to Sally. "Don't laugh, but I don't think I'm going to have much spare time to indulge in any hobbies."

"You're not making any sense. What's going on?"

"I've decided to go back to school, as it were."

Sally's head jutted forward. "You what? And do...?"

"I'm going to become a private investigator."

Sally whooped for joy. "Go you, I couldn't be happier for you. Hey, if you need any tips, I know a couple of people not too far away who I'm sure would be willing to lend a hand."

Lorne hugged Jack. "Good for you. Yep, Tony and I dabbled for a while back in the day. You can bend our ears any time."

"I was hoping you'd say that. Thanks."

Sally raised her glass. "To Jack and Donna and the adventures that lie ahead of them."

THE END

THANK YOU FOR READING SINNER. The next book in this exciting cold case series **The Good Die Young** is now available.

IN THE MEANTIME, have you read any of my other fast paced crime thrillers yet? Why not try the first book in the DI Sara Ramsey series <u>No Right to Kill</u>

OR GRAB the first book in the bestselling, award-winning, Justice series here, <u>Cruel Justice.</u>

OR THE FIRST book in the spin-off Justice Again series, <u>Gone In Seconds.</u>

WHY NOT TRY the first book in the DI Sam Cobbs series, set in the beautiful Lake District, <u>To Die For.</u>

PERHAPS YOU'D PREFER to try one of my other police procedural series, the DI Kayli Bright series which begins with <u>The Missing Children.</u>

. . .

OR MAYBE YOU'D enjoy the DI Sally Parker series set in Norfolk, <u>Wrong Place.</u>

OR MY GRITTY police procedural starring DI Nelson set in Manchester, <u>Torn Apart.</u>

OR MAYBE YOU'D like to try one of my successful psychological thrillers <u>She's Gone</u>, <u>I KNOW THE TRUTH</u> or <u>Shattered Lives.</u>

KEEP IN TOUCH WITH M A COMLEY

Pick up a FREE novella by signing up to my newsletter today.
https://BookHip.com/WBRTGW

BookBub
www.bookbub.com/authors/m-a-comley

Blog

http://melcomley.blogspot.com

Why not join my special Facebook group to take part in monthly giveaways.

Readers' Group